THE RETURN OF NORMANDIE

Our Story So Far...

April Kane is being forced, in a set-up over her brother in India, to help Sam Tapper get information on gold shipments Ryan is involved with, but she manages to tip Pat and Terry that she's in trouble. Pat comes over to her place faking drunkenness and invites Tapper for a drink...

ISBN 0-918348-84-6
LC 87-090446

© NBM 1990
Cover designed and painted by Ray Fehrenbach

Terry & The Pirates is a registered trademark of the Tribune Media Services, Inc.

THE FLYING BUTTRESS
CLASSICS LIBRARY
is an imprint of:

NANTIER·BEALL·MINOUSTCHINE
Publishing co.
new york

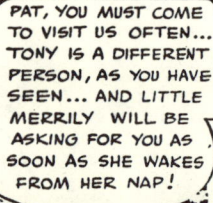

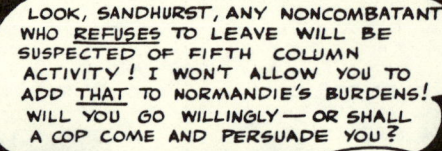

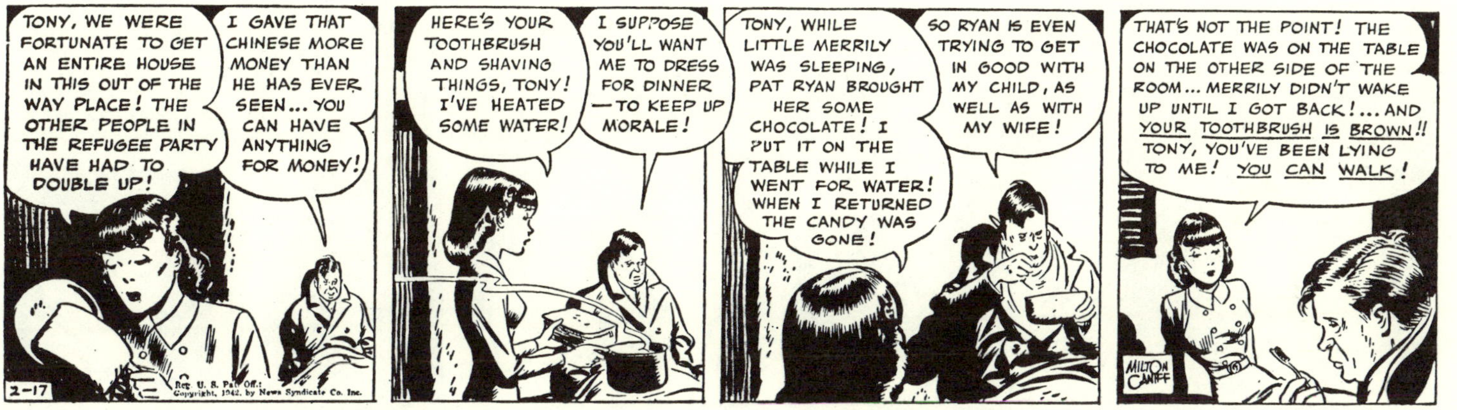

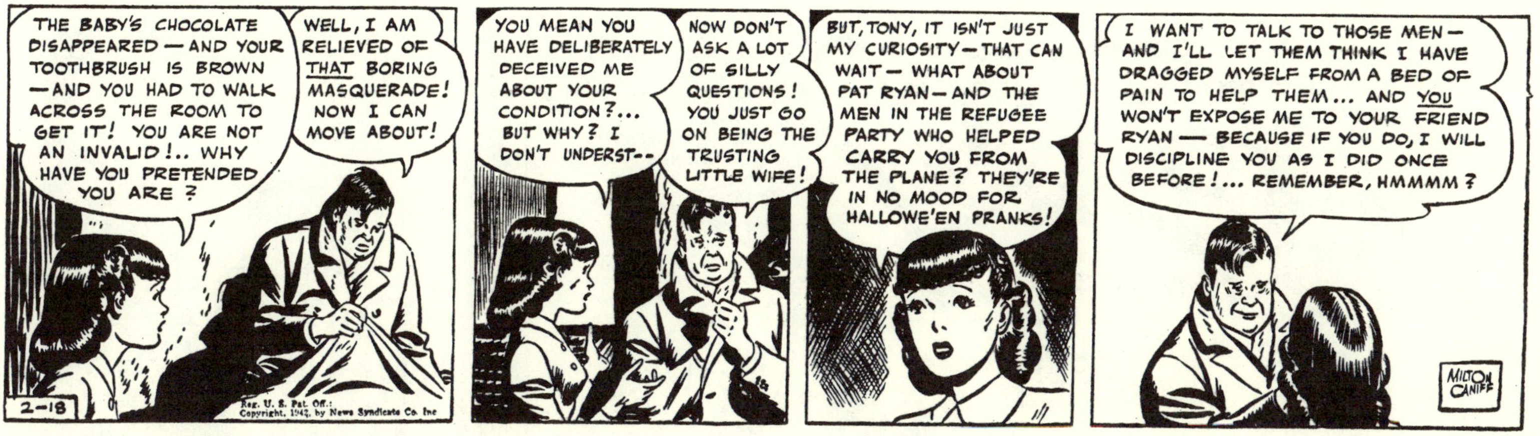

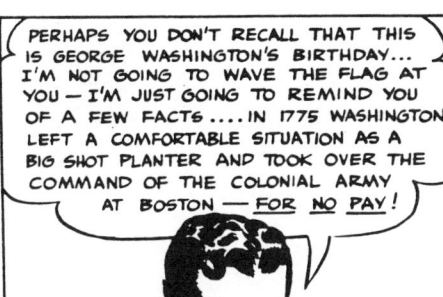

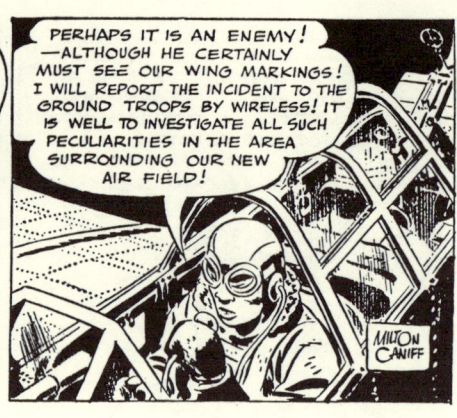

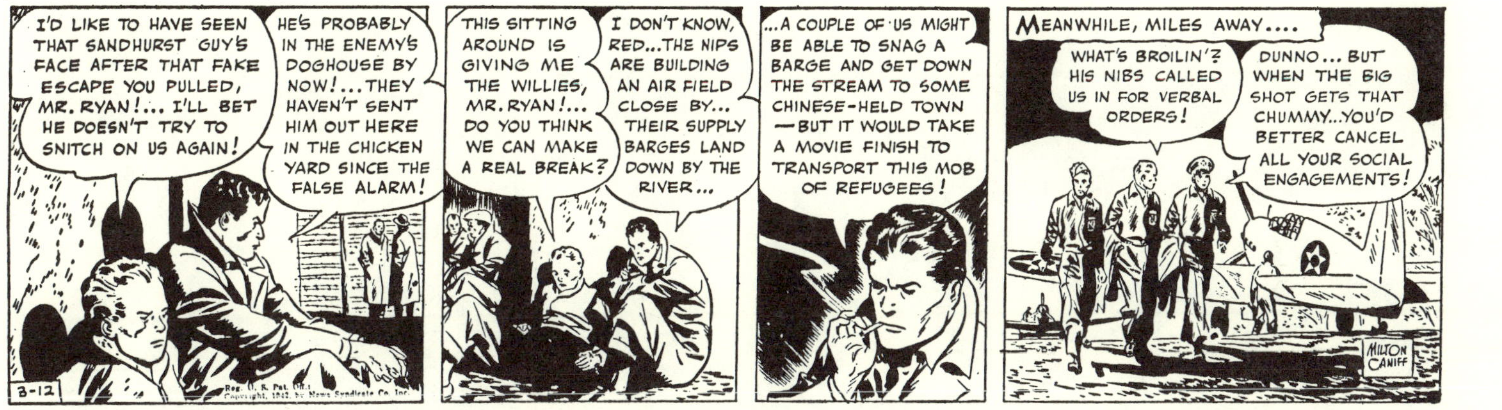

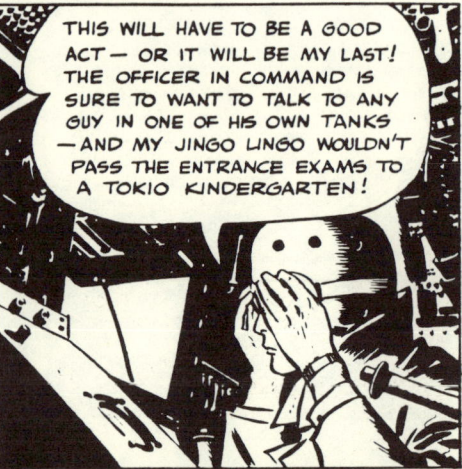

THEY'RE GETTING CLOSER... MAYBE, IF I BUTTONED UP THIS CRIB, I COULD TURN ON THE RADIO TO SOME OF THEIR OWN JABBER! THEY MIGHT THINK A COUPLE OF GENERALS WERE HAVING A CONFERENCE IN HERE!
MEANWHILE, IN A RADIO STATION OF THE BUREAU OF PUBLIC ENLIGHTENMENT...
CHILDREN OF THE SUN EMPEROR, THIS IS YOUR DAILY INSTRUCTION IN THE METHODS OF OUR GLORIOUS ARMED FORCES... WHEN ONE OF OUR COMMANDERS ENCOUNTERS AN ARMY OF THE ENEMY, HE MERELY SENDS A MESSAGE SAYING...
"...THERE WILL BE NO BATTLE!... I, THE MOST BENEVOLENT REPRESENTATIVE OF THE SON OF HEAVEN, ORDER YOU TO ABOUT-FACE AND LEAVE THE FIELD AT ONCE!
...BUT, THERE WAS A REPORT OF SOME PRISONERS ESCAPING...
" IF THIS COMMAND IS NOT OBEYED, THE WRATH OF THE ALL-HIGHEST WILL DESCEND UPON YOU! BE GONE!"
30006
FOR PETE'S SAKE! THEY'RE MOVING AWAY! ...BETTER TURN THIS THING DOWN BEFORE THE OLD BOY TIPS THEM OFF WITH A STATION BREAK!
...OF COURSE, SOME OF THE FOREIGN DEVILS HAVE BEEN SO STUPID THAT THEY TRIED TO FIGHT US...
3-22
...FOR THAT REASON, THE GOVERNMENT IS CUTTING THE SUPPLY OF RICE TO CIVILIANS ...SINCE IT MAY BE SOME TIME BEFORE ALL OF THE ANNOYING INFIDELS ARE DRIVEN FROM ASIA...
OKAY, SUKI YAKI, YOU'VE SERVED YOUR PURPOSE! I DON'T KNOW WHAT YOU'RE SELLING, BUT I'LL SEND YOU THE TOP OFF A BOX OF INCENDIARY BOMBS AT MY EARLIEST OPPORTUNITY!

REFUGEES GOT AWAY—THANKS TO THOSE AMERICAN BOMBERS ...BUT NORMANDIE, MERRILY AND TONY SANDHURST ARE LOCKED IN A BUILDING BACK IN THE VILLAGE... IT WON'T BE A PLEASURE TO HELP RATSY TONY TO ESCAPE!....
3-23
Reg. U. S. Pat. Off.: Copyright, 1942, by News Syndicate Co. Inc.
I THINK WE SLUGGED ALL THE GUARDS... BUT I'LL TAKE NO CHANCES... I RAN THIS CLANK-WAGON OFF THE ROAD AND LEFT THE ENGINE RUNNING... BETTER THROW SOME HAY OVER IT TO PLAY SAFE---
WISH I KNEW WHICH ROOM THEY'RE LOCKED IN...THIS SPOOK PARADING WASTES TIME—BUT I DON'T WANT TO STIR UP ANY NIPPOS WHO MIGHT STILL BE HERE... HEY! WHAT'S THAT?...
MASTER! BEHOLD! THE REFUGEES HAVE DEPARTED —AND THE GUARDS LIE STRICKEN!
STRICKEN WITH LEAD POISONING!... I WILL BE COURT-MARTIALED FOR THIS... QUICKLY! IF SANDHURST AND HIS WIFE ARE STILL LOCKED WHERE WE LEFT THEM ...THEY SHALL BE MY SCAPEGOATS...
MILTON CANIFF

I'M STANDING ON DYNAMITE —WITH A PAIR OF JAPS READY TO GIVE ME A HOT-FOOT! THAT'S THE LIEUTENANT WHO WAS IN CHARGE OF THE REFUGEES...AND HE'S BOILING!... I COULD PICK THEM OFF—BUT THEY'LL LEAD ME TO NORMANDIE, MERRILY AND TONY SANDHURST... I'D BETTER DUCK INTO THE SHADOWS...
3-24
Reg. U. S. Pat. Off.: Copyright, 1942, by News Syndicate Co. Inc.
EVERY GUARD GONE... BUT THE PRISONERS' DOOR IS STILL SECURE! I MUST FINISH THIS BUSINESS QUICKLY!...
THE PRISONERS ARE STILL HERE... SUCCESS!
AH, LIEUTENANT! THERE HAS BEEN SHOOTING—WE DID NOT KNOW WHAT WAS GOING ON!...
...WILL COME TO THE POINT!...WHILE I WAS AWAY, ALL REFUGEES ESCAPED, AFTER SHOOTING SEVERAL OF MY MEN! ...I WILL BE HELD RESPONSIBLE... I WILL TELL MY SUPERIORS BIG ESCAPE SUCCEEDED ONLY WITH THE HELP OF AMERICAN AIRCRAFT AND EXPERT SPY WORK... BUT THAT I CAPTURED THE RINGLEADERS OF VAST PLOT! YOU, MR. AND MRS. SANDHURST, WILL BE MY ALIBI!
MILTON CANIFF

A FINE HOW-HAVE-YOU-BEEN! THAT JAP LIEUTENANT IN THERE SAYS HE WILL USE NORMANDIE AND TONY SANDHURST AS HIS ALIBI FOR ALLOWING THE REFUGEES TO ESCAPE!
3-25
Reg. U. S. Pat. Off.: Copyright, 1942, by News Syndicate Co. Inc.
BUT WE HAD NOTHING TO DO WITH THE ESCAPE... IF YOU TELL YOUR SUPERIORS WE ENGINEERED THE BREAK — WE'LL BE SHOT AS SPIES!
...THAT, MADAM, IS PRECISELY WHAT I HAD IN MIND!
I GUESS THIS HAS GONE FAR ENOUGH!... YOUR ALIBI PLAN IS TRUE IN ITS ESSENTIALS... I DID NOT WISH TO INCRIMINATE MY OWN WIFE — BUT I KNOW I CAN BE OF TOO MUCH VALUE TO YOUR GOVERNMENT TO BE SHOT... SHE ACTUALLY DID ARRANGE THE ESCAPE!
...MRS. SANDHURST IS IN LOVE WITH THE MAN NAMED RYAN!...SHE BRIBED THE GUARD TO ALLOW HER TO SEE RYAN AT ODD MOMENTS...I KNEW THIS, OF COURSE, BUT I KEPT QUIET UNTIL I WAS CERTAIN OF THE DETAILS... YOU LEFT HERE JUST AS I WAS ABOUT TO TELL YOU OF THE PLOT...
MILTON CANIFF
YOU MEAN TO SAY YOU WOULD INCRIMINATE YOUR WIFE IN THE REFUGEE ESCAPE PLOT TO KEEP FROM BEING SHOT YOURSELF?
MIGHT AS WELL BE REALISTIC!...SHE IS IN LOVE WITH RYAN...I CAN BE OF VALUE TO YOUR GOVERNMENT...AND I HAVE POWERFUL FRIENDS THERE...
3-26
Reg. U. S. Pat. Off.: Copyright, 1942, by News Syndicate Co. Inc.
I LEARNED LONG AGO THAT MRS. SANDHURST HAD FOUND OUT MY CONNECTIONS IN TOKIO — AND THAT SHE VOLUNTEERED TO THE UNITED STATES ARMY INTELLIGENCE TO RETURN TO ME TO LEARN WHAT SHE COULD OF MY ACTIVITIES... YOU KNOW HOW INTENSELY PATRIOTIC SOME AMERICAN WOMEN ARE, LIEUTENANT...
MUST CONFESS THAT INCREDIBLE STORY HAS FASCINATED ME INTO INACTIVITY!... HOWEVER, SAME IS NOT BELIEVED... MAN AND WOMAN WILL BE USED AS ALIBI FOR LOSS OF PRISONERS!
YOU'RE A SMART COOKIE, LIEUTENANT! — BUT, SINCE THIS IS A DAY FOR YARN SPINNING, SUPPOSE YOU LISTEN TO A LITTLE PLAN I HAVE IN WHICH YOU ARE THE STOOGE!
MILTON CANIFF
PAT RYAN!
RYAN! YOU'RE JUST IN TIME! I HAD TO TELL THIS LIEUTENANT A TALL STORY TO SAVE THE THREE OF US FROM THE FIRING SQUAD!
MR. RYAN!
I WAS LISTENING OUTSIDE THE DOOR...! NORMANDIE! HAND ME THEIR GUNS! NOW, LIEUTENANT, START WALKING TOWARD THE ENTRANCE!
3-27
Reg. U. S. Pat. Off.: Copyright, 1942, by News Syndicate Co. Inc.
NORMANDIE! TAKE MERRILY AND GET INTO THE TANK YOU WILL FIND ON THE OTHER SIDE OF THE BUILDING! LIEUTENANT, YOU AND YOUR AIDE WILL FACE THE WALL ACROSS THE STREET... WITH YOUR HANDS UP....
DON'T GET FANCY, LIEUTENANT! YOU KNOW HOW EASILY THIS TOMMY GUN WORKS!
BEAUTIFULLY DONE, RYAN! ...WHAT HAPPENS NOW?...
THIS!
MILTON CANIFF
I'VE BEEN WANTING TO SOCK YOU FOR A LONG TIME, SANDHURST — BUT THIS HAS A DOUBLE PURPOSE... DO YOU WANT TO LEAVE IN THE TANK WITH NORMANDIE, MERRILY AND ME?
3-28
Reg. U. S. Pat. Off.: Copyright, 1942, by News Syndicate Co. Inc.
I COULD MOW YOU DOWN, LIEUTENANT — BUT WE DON'T PLAY IT THAT WAY... I'LL SLUG UP YOUR TIRES AND RADIO — AND BID YOU GOOD AFTERNOON...
17
HOLD ON, NORMANDIE AND MERRILY! WE'RE OFF TO NOWHERE!
BUT, PAT... TONY — WHERE IS HE?
MILTON CANIFF
I KNEW YOU'D SAY THAT — IN SPITE OF THE WAY HE BOOTED YOU AROUND! — AFTER YOU CLIMBED INTO THE TANK, I ASKED HIM IF HE WANTED TO GO WITH US... AND HE DIDN'T MAKE A MOVE TO LEAVE....

Reg. U. S. Pat. Off.:
Copyright, 1942, by News Syndicate Co. Inc.
TERRY AND THE PIRATES
BY MILTON CANIFF
OH, PAT, THIS IS AWFUL!
YOU BET IT'S AWFUL, NORMANDIE!
I ADMIRE YOUR LOYALTY IN STICKING TO YOUR HUSBAND, IN SPITE OF EVERYTHING HE'S DONE — BUT YOU HEARD HIM SAY HE'D SACRIFICE YOU TO SAVE HIS OWN PRECIOUS HIDE! THE NIPPOS HAVE TO PUNISH SOMEONE FOR ALLOWING THEIR PRISONERS TO ESCAPE!
BUT TONY IS BACK THERE!... THEY'LL PUNISH HIM!
SANDHURST IS AN EXPERT AT DEALING WITH THE ENEMY... HE'LL DIVERT THEM BY HELPING CATCH US!... WHICH THEY WON'T DO, IF I CAN HELP IT!
IT'S ALL SO FUTILE, PAT! WE MAY HOLD OUT FOR A TIME... BUT WE'RE SO FEW —AND THEY ARE SO MANY...
THAT DOESN'T SOUND LIKE YOU, NORMANDIE! YOU KNOW VERY WELL WHAT HAPPENS TO WOMEN PRISONERS! ...YOU WEREN'T HARMED BEFORE BECAUSE YOUR HUSBAND HAD CONNECTIONS WITH THE AXIS... — HEY! HEAR THAT?
AIRPLANE..! —OH, PAT, THEY'RE AFTER US!
...THEY'LL TRY TO HEAD US OFF, TOO! —AND THIS JIGGLE WAGON WON'T RUN FOREVER WITHOUT GASOLINE!...
WH-WHY, PAT, THEY DIDN'T FIRE A SHOT!... DO YOU SUPPOSE THEY'RE JUST TRYING TO LOCATE US?
YOU'RE RIGHT, NORMANDIE! TANKS COST TOO MUCH FOR THEM TO DESTROY THEIR OWN WITH BOMBS! IT WOULD BE CHEAPER TO CUT US OFF! THEY COULD STARVE US OUT EVENTUALLY... BUT WE'LL TRY EVERYTHING FIRST...
BEHOLD! THE YANKEE FUGITIVE THINKS HE ESCAPES US BY HIDING AMONG THE TREES! —HE DOES NOT KNOW HOW CLEAR TANK TRACKS APPEAR FROM THE AIR! SUMMON THE GROUND TROOPS BY WIRELESS!
THE TRACKS ARE CLEAR... JUST AS THE OBSERVATION PLANE REPORTED! APPROACH THE TANK CAREFULLY! THE YANKEE WILL BE DESPERATE... BUT OUR ORDERS ARE TO CAPTURE THE FIRE CART INTACT!...
THE FOOL THINKS HE HAS CAMOUFLAGED THE TANK WITH BRANCHES! CRAWL TO THE SPOT AND GET UNDER HIS GUNS!
?!
We don't make the same Pearl Harbor twice
Love, Yehudi
....AND MY POOR MOM USED TO TELL ME THOSE COWBOY AND INDIAN STORIES I READ IN BED WOULD NEVER DO ME ANY GOOD!
3-29

THE NIPS ARE HOT AFTER US, NORMANDIE! THEIR PATROL PLANES HAVE REPORTED OUR GENERAL LOCATION...
3-30
Reg. U. S. Pat. Off.: Copyright, 1942, by News Syndicate Co. Inc.
...BUT WE HAVE A MARGIN OF SAFETY IN THAT THEY CAN'T SPARE A MOB OF VEHICLES TO CHASE US —AND THEY WON'T DESTROY THIS VALUABLE TANK IF THEY CAN HELP IT!... HEY! WHY THE TEARS?
STILL WORRIED ABOUT YOUR HUSBAND?... I WON'T TRY TO KEEP FROM SAYING HOW I FEEL ABOUT ANY SO-AND-SO WHO WOULD TREAT HIS WIFE AND CHILD AS HE DID!... I ASKED HIM IF HE WANTED TO COME WITH US — AND HE DIDN'T MOVE...
MILTON CANIFF
YOU MEAN HE COULDN'T MOVE! ... AFTER ALL, PAT, EVEN I KNOW WHAT IT MEANS WHEN A MAN'S KNUCKLES ARE RAW!

WE HAD TO LEAVE TOO QUICKLY TO CARRY FOOD, MERRILY, DARLING! WE'LL FIND SOME IN THE MORNING... SLEEP TIGHT!
...I'M HUNGRY, MUZZ!
3-31
Reg. U. S. Pat. Off.: Copyright, 1942, by News Syndicate Co. Inc.
SORE AT ME, NORMANDIE? ...I'LL ADMIT I SOCKED YOUR HUSBAND —BUT, HONEY, HE---
I KNOW WHY YOU DID IT, PAT! TONY IS A TRAITOR —THAT'S PROVED! ...WHAT HE DID TO ME ISN'T IMPORTANT!
IT'S IMPORTANT TO ME! I'M NOT GOING TO ALLOW THE ONLY GIRL I EVER LOVED TO BE KICKED AROUND —EVEN BY HER OWN HUSBAND!
TONY IS ILL, PAT... AND I PROMISED TO 'LOVE AND CHERISH HIM'...'IN SICKNESS AND IN HEALTH'
SICKNESS, MY EYE! THAT BOZO IS AS HEALTHY AS A PRIZE HEIFER AT A COUNTY FAIR!
BIG, SELF-RELIANT FELLOWS LIKE YOU NEVER UNDERSTAND SUCH THINGS, PAT... SOME MEN NEED MOTHERING AS LONG AS THEY LIVE! TONY IS ONE OF THEM— AND I'VE CONTRACTED TO DO THE JOB!
MILTON CANIFF

WHAT IRONY!... I TAKE YOU AND MERRILY AWAY FROM SANDHURST BECAUSE HE WAS KICKING YOU AROUND... NOW YOU TELL ME YOUR HUSBAND IS JUST A POOR, SICK LITTLE FELLER WHO NEEDS A MOTHER'S CARE! WHY DIDN'T HE GO BACK TO HIS MAMMA — INSTEAD OF MARRYING THE GIRL I LOVE?
4-1
Reg. U. S. Pat. Off.: Copyright, 1942, by News Syndicate Co. Inc.
I'M NOT DEFENDING TONY, PAT! I'M AWARE OF HIS WEAKNESSES... THE POINT IS, I DID MARRY HIM... AND I MEAN TO KEEP THE BARGAIN... HOWEVER ONE-SIDED IT IS... AFTER ALL, THERE'S MERRILY TO CONSIDER!
YEAH! HOW A GLUNK LIKE SANDHURST COULD BE THE FATHER OF SUCH A SWEET KID IS BEYOND ME...
MILTON CANIFF
ARE YOU SURE YOU'D BE SO IN LOVE WITH ME AFTER ALL THESE YEARS IF I HAD POPPED BACK INTO YOUR LIFE, SINGLE, AND WITHOUT A CHILD?·ISN'T YOUR PRIDE HURT BECAUSE ANOTHER MAN GOT YOUR GIRL AND IS THE FATHER OF A CHILD WHO APPEALS TO YOU?
THAT'S A LEADING QUESTION... AND I'LL GIVE YOU A STRAIGHT ANSWER! ...SIT DOWN!

SO, NORMANDIE DRAKE SANDHURST, YOU THINK PERHAPS MY PRIDE IS HURT BECAUSE SANDHURST MARRIED YOU AND BECAME THE FATHER OF SUCH A SWEET CHILD AS MERRILY...
DO YOU REMEMBER WHEN I FIRST MET YOU, YEARS AGO? YOU WERE THE SPOILED NIECE OF A RICH MAN...
4-2
Reg. U. S. Pat. Off.: Copyright, 1942, by News Syndicate Co. Inc.
I SAW YOU TRY TO LIVE UP TO THE MONEY AND SOCIAL POSITION —BUT IN SPITE OF YOURSELF YOU COULDN'T HIDE YOUR GENUINE NATURE! I FELL IN LOVE WITH YOU BECAUSE YOU WERE SWEET AND GENTLE! WE WERE ABOUT TO BE MARRIED WHEN YOUR AUNT SNATCHED YOU AWAY—SO YOU WOULDN'T MARRY A 'BEACHCOMBER'!
IN NEW YORK YOU WENT THROUGH WITH A WEDDING YOUR AUNT ARRANGED WITH A 'PROPER' FAMILY AND YOU DID IT BECAUSE YOU WERE BEHOLDEN TO YOUR AUNT AND UNCLE FOR SUPPORTING YOU...
THE NEXT TIME WE MET, SANDHURST WAS ABOUT TO LEAVE YOU FLAT....ON THE EVE OF THE BIRTH OF YOUR BABY —AND YET YOU DEFENDED HIM! DON'T YOU SEE?... EVERYTHING YOU'VE DONE SINCE CONFIRMS MY ORIGINAL ESTIMATE —THAT YOU'RE THOROUGHBRED... AND YOU'RE STILL BEAUTIFUL... AND I LOVE YOU FOR THE VERY COCKEYED THING THAT MAKES ME SO MAD!... NOW GO TO BED — BEFORE I TRY TO KISS YOU—AND MAKE IT WORSE!
MILTON CANIFF

DID YOU THINK ABOUT THE TALK WE HAD LAST NIGHT, NORMANDIE?
I SAW THE DAWN THIS MORNING... AND IT WASN'T BECAUSE MY ALARM WENT OFF EARLY, PAT!... BUT REMEMBER THAT LITTLE EARS HAVE A WIDE RANGE OF SELECTIVITY!
4-3
Reg. U. S. Pat. Off.: Copyright, 1942, by News Syndicate Co. Inc.
SORRY!...I'M NOT USED TO EDITING MY CONVERSATION ... HEY! HEAR THAT SPUTTER?
THAT MEANT OUT-OF-GAS, BACK IN ANCIENT HISTORY— WHEN I DROVE A CAR!
IT MEANS THE SAME IN ONE OF THESE JALLOPIES! I HAVE A LITTLE JOB TO DO —THEN WE POUND THE LEATHER!
WHAT DO YOU MEAN, PAT?
WHEN SOLDIERS COME UPON AN EMPTY TANK THEY EXAMINE IT FOR PLANTED EXPLOSIVES!... I ATTACHED A GRENADE TO THE STARTER FOR THEM TO FIND... BUT I BURIED THE OTHER BOMBS IN THE ROAD... UNDER THE TREADS... WITH A WIRE FROM TREADS TO FIRING PINS! WHEN THE TANK MOVES — THE PINS WILL BE PULLED — AND SEVERAL NIPPOS WILL LOSE INTEREST IN THE WAR!
MILTON CANIFF

PAT, WOULD YOU HATE ME IF I SAID I HAVE TO GIVE UP?
DON'T BLAME YOU, NORMANDIE!... I'VE BEEN TRYING TO REACH THE RIVER — AND I THINK I SEE IT THROUGH THE TREES! A BOAT IS OUR ONLY CHANCE, NOW!
4-4
Reg. U. S. Pat. Off.: Copyright, 1942, by News Syndicate Co. Inc.
NOW I KNOW HOW A SLEEP-WALKER FEELS!
THIS BURNED VILLAGE SEEMS ABANDONED... WE'LL CRAWL IN OUT OF SIGHT AND GET SOME REST!
PAT, WE'VE GOT TO FIND SOME FOOD FOR MERRILY!
...AND YOU DON'T LOOK OVERSTUFFED YOURSELF, HONEY! PARK IN THIS HUT! I'LL RUSTLE SOME GRUB WHEN IT'S LIGHT ENOUGH...
MILTON CANIFF

Reg. U. S. Pat. Off.: Copyright, 1942, by News Syndicate Co. Inc.
TERRY AND THE PIRATES
by MILTON CANIFF
HOW DO YOU FEEL, NORMANDIE?
I THINK I'M A SISSY, PAT!
YOU'RE A THOROUGHBRED IN MY BOOK, HONEY... AND SO IS MERRILY! I'M GLAD SHE'S MORE LIKE YOU THAN HER FATHER!
OH, PAT, THAT'S UNKIND!
SORRY! I GUESS IT'S PART OF BEING A THOROUGHBRED TO KEEP A BARGAIN — EVEN IF IT'S BAD!... I WISH WE HADN'T HAD TO GIVE UP OUR TANK... I WAS GETTING FOND OF THAT FUJIYAMA FLIVVER!
THIS IS BETTER THAN BEING CAPTURED... BUT, PAT, THEY WILL FIND US EVENTUALLY... I CAN'T HELP THINKING...
NOW, LOOK, BEAUTIFUL, WE'RE NOT IN JAIL UNTIL WE HEAR THE KEY TURN BEHIND US!... THIS VILLAGE IS DESERTED... WE WILL LOOK FOR FOOD IN THE MORNING!... YOU SLEEP FOR AWHILE SO YOU WILL HAVE SOME STRENGTH...
FOR HOURS PAT FIGHTS SLEEP... THEN EXHAUSTION TAKES ITS TOLL... HE NODS...

PAT!
...FELL ASLEEP... BUT I HAVE HIM COVERED! ...HE MAY BE AN ENEMY SPY, POSING AS A CHINESE TO TRACK US DOWN!...
DON'T TRY TO MOVE! IF THERE ARE ENEMY SOLDIERS OUTSIDE, YOU'LL GET IT BEFORE THEY TAKE US!
PAT! HE'S POINTING TO HIS FEET!
4-5
RELAX, NORMANDIE! HE'S SHOWING HIS IDENTIFICATION!...IF HE WERE JAPANESE HE'D HAVE A WIDE SPACE BETWEEN HIS FIRST AND SECOND TOES — FROM WEARING SINGLE-STRAP SANDALS SINCE CHILDHOOD! CHINESE WEAR SLIPPERS — OR GO BAREFOOT!...THERE'S AN ALLY IN OUR ALLEY!

SPEAK BIG ENGLISH, ME!
SWELL... I HOPE YOU AREN'T ANGRY BECAUSE I SLAPPED A GUN ON YOU WHEN YOU CAUGHT ME NAPPING JUST NOW!...WE THOUGHT YOU MIGHT BE A JAP SPY!...IF YOUR FEET DIDN'T SHOW THAT YOU HADN'T WORN JAPANESE SANDALS AS A CHILD, I WOULD STILL BE IN DOUBT!
4-6
Reg. U.S. Pat. Off.: Copyright, 1942, by News Syndicate Co. Inc.
WE'RE ABOUT THREE JUMPS AHEAD OF THE ENEMY PATROLS... IS THERE ANY FOOD TO BE HAD AROUND HERE?
...OH, CERTAIN IS! GOT PLENTY!
YOU'LL PARDON MY CURIOSITY — BUT I SEE NOTHING AROUND HERE BUT THE SHELL OF A BURNED VILLAGE
MILTON CANIFF
MUCH SECRET! — BUT WILL SHOW! ...PLACE WILL B'LONG ALL SAME LIKE HOME TO WANDERING PAPA, MAMA AND SMALL GIRL-CHILD!

...IS TRAPPED DOOR IN FALL-DOWN HOUSE! ME LONG TIME LIVE SAME PLACE... FIX GOOD TO HIDE FLOM JAP NOSEYBODY!
AFTER YOU!
4-7
Reg. U.S. Pat. Off.: Copyright, 1942, by News Syndicate Co. Inc.
HA! PLENTY CAREFUL... BUT NO WORRIES!... NIP-NIP NO B'LONG SPY!
OH, PAT, LOOK! IT'S A COMPLETE APARTMENT!
WELL, MR. NIP-NIP, WE CERTAINLY APPRECIATE YOUR HOSPITALITY... BUT ISN'T IT DANGEROUS FOR YOU TO BRING COMPLETE STRANGERS TO YOUR HIDING PLACE?
MEBBE NIP-NIP SOFT IN HEART...OR MEBBE IN HEAD — BUT NIP-NIP ALSO GOT WIFE AN' SMALL GIRL-CHILD — NOW PRISONERS OF JAPS! GOT SYMPATHY FOR MAN WITH FAMILY!
MILTON CANIFF

... NIP-NIP MAKE SUDDEN HURRY TEA AN' EAT THINGS FOR MAMA, PAPA AN' GIRL-CHILD!
PAT, THIS IS DIFFICULT! THAT AMAZING LITTLE MAN SEEMS TO HAVE TAKEN US IN BECAUSE HE THINKS I AM YOUR WIFE AND MERRILY IS YOUR DAUGHTER ... AND IT REMINDS HIM OF HIS OWN WIFE AND CHILD ...
4-8
Reg. U. S. Pat. Off.: Copyright, 1942, by News Syndicate Co. Inc.
HE'S GETTING SUCH A BOOT OUT OF IT... I HATE TO TELL HIM! FOR THAT MATTER, I WISH IT WERE TRUE!... I'LL TAKE HIM ASIDE AFTER WE EAT!.. HERE COMES THE GRUB!
HMM — GOOD!
MUZZ! THE CHINESE PEOPLE ARE SO NICE TO US... WHY WAS DADDY SO VERY FRIENDLY WITH THOSE JAPANESE SOLDIERS?
MILTON CANIFF

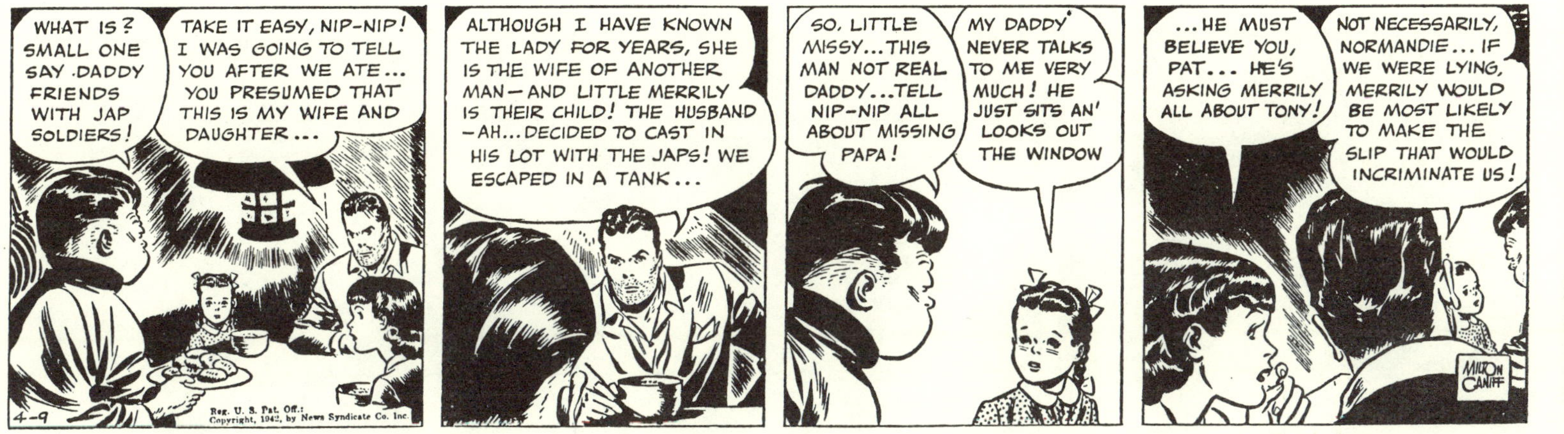
WHAT IS? SMALL ONE SAY DADDY FRIENDS WITH JAP SOLDIERS!
TAKE IT EASY, NIP-NIP! I WAS GOING TO TELL YOU AFTER WE ATE... YOU PRESUMED THAT THIS IS MY WIFE AND DAUGHTER...
4-9
Reg. U. S. Pat. Off.: Copyright, 1942, by News Syndicate Co. Inc.
ALTHOUGH I HAVE KNOWN THE LADY FOR YEARS, SHE IS THE WIFE OF ANOTHER MAN — AND LITTLE MERRILY IS THEIR CHILD! THE HUSBAND — AH... DECIDED TO CAST IN HIS LOT WITH THE JAPS! WE ESCAPED IN A TANK...
SO, LITTLE MISSY... THIS MAN NOT REAL DADDY... TELL NIP-NIP ALL ABOUT MISSING PAPA!
MY DADDY NEVER TALKS TO ME VERY MUCH! HE JUST SITS AN' LOOKS OUT THE WINDOW
... HE MUST BELIEVE YOU, PAT... HE'S ASKING MERRILY ALL ABOUT TONY!
NOT NECESSARILY, NORMANDIE... IF WE WERE LYING, MERRILY WOULD BE MOST LIKELY TO MAKE THE SLIP THAT WOULD INCRIMINATE US!
MILTON CANIFF

...SO, LITTLE ONE, BIG MISSY B'LONG MAMA — BUT MAN IS NOT REAL PAPA! TELL MORE ABOUT MISSING DADDY!
... MY DADDY WAS AWAY FOR A LONG TIME... MUZZ AND I CAME ON A BIG BOAT TO SEE HIM! HE WAS SICK AND COULDN'T WALK!
4-10
Reg. U. S. Pat. Off.: Copyright, 1942, by News Syndicate Co. Inc.
TELL NIP-NIP WHAT REAL DADDY LOOK LIKE!
MY DADDY IS SORT OF FAT... HE SAT IN A WHEEL-CHAIR AND HAD BROWN HAIR THAT WOULDN'T STAY COMBED! HE WAS ANGRY WHEN I PLAYED TRAIN IN THE HALL!
MY DADDY SAID THINGS THAT MADE MUZZ CRY ...'SPECIALLY AFTER MR. RYAN CAME TO OUR HOUSE! MR. RYAN PULLED AMAH AND ME FROM IN FRONT OF A BIG TANK!..
MY DADDY WAS VERY ANGRY WITH MR. RYAN BECAUSE MR. RYAN LIKES MY MUZZ!... I KNOW HE LIKES HER, TOO... BECAUSE HE KISSED HER ONE NIGHT WHEN MUZZ WAS ASLEEP — AND HE THOUGHT I WAS!
MILTON CANIFF

...WHAT ELSE DO YOU WANT TO KNOW ABOUT MY DADDY, MR. NIP-NIP?
IS ENOUGH, LITTLE MISSY! MEBBE NOW GO SLEEP TIME!
YES, YOU SHOULD BE IN BED, MERRILY!
4-11
Reg. U. S. Pat. Off.: Copyright, 1942, by News Syndicate Co. Inc.
NIP-NIP, COULDN'T WE HANG THAT MAT ACROSS THE ROOM TO GIVE NORMANDIE AND MERRILY SOME PRIVACY?
IS SO! WILL DO!
WELL, NIP-NIP, IT WAS A NEAT TRICK TO ASK THE CHILD ABOUT HER FATHER, RATHER THAN TAKING OUR WORD THAT HE WENT OVER TO THE JAPS! YOU'RE SMARTER THAN JUST A FARMER-REFUGEE FROM THE INVADER!
MILTON CANIFF
... MEBBE SO, MEBBE SO! SMART ENOUGH TO SEE THAT — EVEN THOUGH PAPA OF SMALL ONE FOOLISH ENOUGH TO GO WITH JAPS — CERTAIN MELICAN FELLA GOT PLENTY REASON TO ENVY HIM — FOR OTHER THINGS!... IS SO?
YEA, VERILY!

Reg. U. S. Pat. Off.:
Copyright, 1942, by News Syndicate Co. Inc.
TERRY AND THE PIRATES
by MILTON CANIFF
NIP-NIP, WE'RE VERY GRATEFUL TO YOU FOR HIDING US FROM THE ENEMY IN THIS EMPTY VILLAGE ... BY THE WAY, HOW DID YOU GET THAT ODD NAME?
NIP-NIP CALLED SAME BY MELICANS, SHANGHAI-SIDE! NIP-NIP EXPERT JAP-SLAP! .... MAKE PLENTY NO FUN FOR LITTLE SUN RISERS! ... NIP-NIP COME TO HOME VILLAGE FOR HEALTH... AFTER BOMB MYSTERIOUSLY EXPLODE IN ENEMY GENERAL TEA POT!
BUT HOW DO YOU KNOW WE ARE NOT AXIS AGENTS?
NIP-NIP RAISE HAND, LIKE SO, SAY 'HEIL HITLERINI'... TO SMALL MISSY!... SHE THINK NIP-NIP SWEAR AN' POINT AT UNSEEN PERSON! IF PAPA AN' MAMA AXERS— SMALL CHILD SURE TO BE MAKE-LEARN SALUTE—SO PARENTS NO FEEL SO SILLY DOING SAME!.... NIP-NIP GO NOW, GOT BUSY!
OKAY, NIP-NIP! WE'LL HOLD THE FORT!
THE STRANGE LITTLE MAN LIES NEAR THE MAIN ROAD WHILE SEVERAL UNITS OF MECHANIZED TROOPS GO BY... THEN, A SINGLE TANK, WHICH HAS FALLEN BEHIND FOR MINOR REPAIRS, APPEARS DOWN THE VALLEY....
NIP-NIP HASTILY MOVES THE ARMY ROAD MARKER, CAUSING IT TO POINT DOWN THE OPPOSITE FORK... THEN HE SCAMPERS AHEAD ALONG THE DETOUR...
AT A BRIDGE OVER A DEEP STREAM, NIP-NIP REMOVES A SINGLE LOG.... THEN HIDES IN THE BRUSH...
SOON THE TANK, OBEYING THE FALSE MARKER, RUMBLES UP TO THE BRIDGEHEAD....
ACCURSED BRIDGE!... TEST FOR MINES!
WITH A METEORITE DETECTOR TO LOCATE BURIED METAL, THE SOLDIER SOUNDS OUT THE SPAN FOR HIDDEN EXPLOSIVES....
ALL IS WELL! PROCEED!
FOR HALF ITS LENGTH, THE BRIDGE CARRIES THE TANK EASILY.... THEN....
4-12
YOU WEREN'T GONE LONG, NIP-NIP! DID YOU MEET ANY OF OUR LITTLE FRIENDS?
IS SO! TODAY PLAY 'SEE-SAW, MARGIE DAWSON' ... DON'T THINK TOOTHY ONES LIKE GAME SO GOOD!

WHAT DO YOU THINK ABOUT THIS NIP-NIP CHAP, PAT?.... CAN WE TRUST HIM?
WE HAVEN'T MUCH CHOICE, NORMANDIE... HE SEEMS TO ENJOY OUR COMPANY...
4-13
Reg. U. S. Pat. Off.: Copyright, 1942, by News Syndicate Co. Inc.
HE COULD CERTAINLY DO US HARM IF HE CHOSE! WHY DO YOU SUPPOSE HE'S IN THIS OUT-OF-THE-WAY SPOT?
HE SAID HE GOT THE NAME 'NIP-NIP' BECAUSE HE WAS SO GOOD AT HECKLING THE JAPS...
HE'S PROBABLY ONE OF THE THOUSANDS OF CHINESE GUERILLAS WORKING BEHIND THE INVADERS' LINES... IT'S NOT SMART TO ASK TOO MANY QUESTIONS!
I WONDER WHERE HE IS NOW?
MEANWHILE...
...WE SAW FOREIGNERS... A MAN, WOMAN AND CHILD! IS IT NOW SAFE TO APPROACH?
THIS PERSON HAS THE THREE VISITORS WELL IN HAND!... YOU MAY PROCEED TO THE USUAL PLACE OF STORAGE!
MILTON CANIFF

YOU HAVE DONE WELL! THE HIGH COMMAND SHALL LEARN OF YOUR EFFORTS!...
WE DO NOT SEEK FAME, MY FRIEND! IT IS ENOUGH THAT WE DO EVEN A SMALL THING TO BRING FINAL VICTORY!
4-14
Reg. U. S. Pat. Off.: Copyright, 1942, by News Syndicate Co. Inc.
THIS LAST DELIVERY FILLS ALL AVAILABLE SPACE IN THE CONVEYANCE!... AFTER FINAL ADJUSTMENTS, THIS PERSON DEPARTS!
IT IS HOPED THAT THE FATES DEAL KINDLY WITH THE ENTERPRISE!
WE GO!
MEANWHILE: AT NIP-NIP'S HUT
PAT, I'VE BEEN THINKING...
I SUPPOSE IT'S TOUGH TO GET YOUR HUSBAND OFF YOUR MIND, NORMANDIE... ...I DON'T WA--
...IT ISN'T ABOUT THAT... I'VE BEEN WATCHING YOU... YOU'RE LIKE A FIRE HORSE LEFT BEHIND WHEN THE ALARM RINGS! YOU FEEL YOU SHOULD BE ON THE FRONT LINE—BUT YOU ARE BURDENED WITH MERRILY AND ME! SHE AND I ARE GOING TO MOVE ON!
MILTON CANIFF

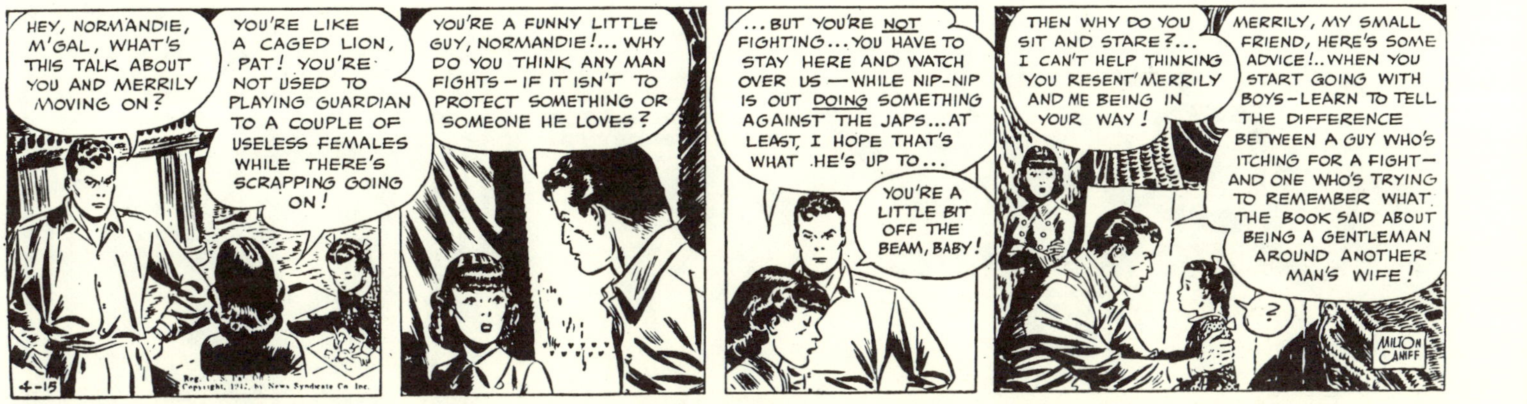
HEY, NORMANDIE, M'GAL, WHAT'S THIS TALK ABOUT YOU AND MERRILY MOVING ON?
YOU'RE LIKE A CAGED LION, PAT! YOU'RE NOT USED TO PLAYING GUARDIAN TO A COUPLE OF USELESS FEMALES WHILE THERE'S SCRAPPING GOING ON!
4-15
Reg. U. S. Pat. Off.: Copyright, 1942, by News Syndicate Co. Inc.
YOU'RE A FUNNY LITTLE GUY, NORMANDIE!... WHY DO YOU THINK ANY MAN FIGHTS—IF IT ISN'T TO PROTECT SOMETHING OR SOMEONE HE LOVES?
...BUT YOU'RE NOT FIGHTING... YOU HAVE TO STAY HERE AND WATCH OVER US—WHILE NIP-NIP IS OUT DOING SOMETHING AGAINST THE JAPS... AT LEAST, I HOPE THAT'S WHAT HE'S UP TO...
YOU'RE A LITTLE BIT OFF THE BEAM, BABY!
THEN WHY DO YOU SIT AND STARE?... I CAN'T HELP THINKING YOU RESENT MERRILY AND ME BEING IN YOUR WAY!
MERRILY, MY SMALL FRIEND, HERE'S SOME ADVICE!.. WHEN YOU START GOING WITH BOYS—LEARN TO TELL THE DIFFERENCE BETWEEN A GUY WHO'S ITCHING FOR A FIGHT—AND ONE WHO'S TRYING TO REMEMBER WHAT THE BOOK SAID ABOUT BEING A GENTLEMAN AROUND ANOTHER MAN'S WIFE!
?
MILTON CANIFF

MERRILY, DARLING, IT'S TIME YOU WERE IN BED! SAY GOOD-NIGHT TO MR. RYAN...
OH, WELL, I GUESS YOU AND MR. RYAN WERE GOING TO START SPELLING WORDS PRETTY SOON, ANYWAY!
COME HERE, YOU PRETTY THING...
4-16
Reg. U. S. Pat. Off.: Copyright, 1942, by News Syndicate Co. Inc.
MERRILY, HAVE I KNOWN YOU LONG ENOUGH TO HOLD YOU VERY TIGHTLY AND TELL YOU HOW SWEET YOU ARE... AND WOULD YOU THINK IT WAS WRONG FOR ME TO KISS YOU?
OH, NO, MR. RYAN, I THINK YOU'RE WONDERFUL!
MR. RYAN WHISPERED IN MY EAR TO HURRY AND KISS YOU BEFORE THE FIRE DIED DOWN! WHAT DID HE MEAN, MUZZ?
MILTON CANIFF

...PAT RYAN, YOU WERE A MEANIE TO MAKE POOR LITTLE MERRILY A PARTY TO THAT KISSING TRICK!
...WELL, I CAN'T KISS YOU—SO I RELAYED IT VIA MERRILY... WE HAVE TO WORK OUT SUBSTITUTES FOR EVERYTHING THESE DAYS...
4-17
Reg. U. S. Pat. Off.: Copyright, 1942, by News Syndicate Co. Inc.
OH, PAT, YOU MAKE A JOKE OF ALL THIS—BUT CAN'T YOU SEE HOW IT'S TORTURING ME? WHY DO YOU THINK I SUGGESTED THAT MERRILY AND I GO AWAY? DO YOU THINK I DON'T REMEMBER WHAT IT WAS LIKE TO HAVE YOU HOLD ME IN YOUR ARMS AND TELL ME YOU LOVE ME?
MILTON CANIFF

WHILE NORMANDIE AND PAT RYAN WONDER ABOUT THE ACTIVITIES OF THE CHINESE CALLED NIP-NIP.... A SHARP MILITARY ACTION IS IN PROGRESS NEAR THE CHINA COAST
4-18
Reg. U. S. Pat. Off.: Copyright, 1942, by News Syndicate Co. Inc.
THE EXPLOSION WAS NOT GREAT ENOUGH TO WRECK THE OIL TANKS, MY COMMANDER!
I FEARED THAT! FALL BACK BEFORE WE ARE WIPED OUT!
IF NIP-NIP HAD ARRIVED THIS WOULD NEVER HAVE HAPPENED! A CURSE ON THE DELAYS!
THE LAST ATTACKER HAS BEEN DRIVEN OFF... IS THE CAPTAIN BADLY WOUNDED?
...NOT SO BADLY PHYSICALLY AS MENTALLY!... THE BLOW WAS DELIVERED BY A WOMAN!
MILTON CANIFF

TERRY AND THE PIRATES
by MILTON CANIFF
NORMANDIE, WE'VE BEEN LUCKY... THIS FUNNY NIP-NIP TOOK US IN WHEN WE HARDLY HAD A CHANCE OF SURVIVAL... BUT HE BOTHERS ME A BIT...
...HE PRACTICALLY ADOPTED US AFTER WE SLIPPED AWAY FROM THE ENEMY... BUT HE IS NO ORDINARY COOLIE...
I'VE NOTICED IT TOO, PAT!... HE SAYS HE CAME BACK TO HIS NATIVE VILLAGE TO HECKLE THE JAPS... BUT HE IS FAR FROM BEING A SIMPLE FARM BOY!
...HELLO, MR. NIP-NIP ... WHY DO YOU HAVE THAT BIG KNIFE?
OH, IT IS YOU, LITTLE ONE...

OF COURSE IT'S ME... MERRILY! WHY DO YOU LOOK SO FUNNY, MR. NIP-NIP?
THE SMALL ONE SURPRISED ME... I WAS—BUSY! I THOUGHT YOU WERE SOME OTHER PERSON....
OH, MY MUZZ AND MR. RYAN ARE THE ONLY OTHER PEOPLE HERE... AND THEY WOULDN'T ROMP AROUND THE RIVER... 'CAUSE YOU ASKED THEM NOT TO...
IS THAT SO, LITTLE MERRILY... DID YOUR MOTHER AND MR. RYAN SAY ANYTHING ELSE ABOUT NIP-NIP?
MR. RYAN SAID HE THINKS YOU AREN'T JUST A FARMER... BUT HE SAYS YOU WERE NICE TO US —AND WE SHOULDN'T TRY TO BOTHER YOU IN WHATEVER YOU'RE DOING!... WHAT ARE YOU DOING MR. NIP-NIP?
...WHAT AM I DOING, GIRL-CHILD? ...THAT IS A LONG STORY... BUT WHAT YOU SAY ABOUT MR. RYAN CAUSES ME TO MAKE A DECISION! COME ALONG, LITTLE ONE!

SAY, MR. NIP-NIP —YOU DON'T TALK FUNNY LIKE BEFORE! ...YOU SAY THINGS RIGHT— JUST LIKE MY MUZZ AND DADDY AND MR. RYAN...
...THE LITTLE MERRILY IS MOST OBSERVANT... YES, NIP-NIP KNOWS YOUR LANGUAGE...AND HE MUST SPEAK SOME OF IT TO YOUR MR. RYAN... TIME GROWS UNCOMFORTABLY SHORT...
AS MERRILY AND NIP-NIP GO TO TALK TO PAT... ANOTHER SCENE IS TAKING PLACE MILES AWAY...
DID FORTUNE SMILE UPON OUR EFFORTS THIS TIME, MY COMMANDER?
FORTUNE LAUGHED ALOUD AT OUR LACK OF EXPLOSIVES! IS THERE WORD OF THE LONG ABSENT NIP-NIP?
4-19
MY COMMANDER WILL RECALL THAT THE MISSION OF NIP-NIP WAS ONE OF GREAT DANGER! HE MAY HAVE FAILED!...
NIP-NIP IS SMART... HE MUST HAVE BEEN DELAYED BY SOME INCIDENT OF IMPORTANCE ...HE KNOWS WHAT THE DRAGON LADY DOES TO DAWDLERS!

4-20
Reg. U. S. Pat. Off.; Copyright, 1942, by News Syndicate Co. Inc
MERRILY, DARLING, I JUST NOTICED YOU WEREN'T PLAYING BY THE DOOR! MUZZ WAS WORRIED! WHERE HAVE YOU BEEN?
IT WAS A PRETTY DAY... AND I WENT TO THE RIVER... AND I FOUND MR. NIP-NIP IN A HOUSE THERE ...AND HE HAD A BIG KNIFE... AND HE DIDN'T TALK THE SAME...AND--
A KNIFE? WHAT IS ALL THIS?
PERHAPS I HAD BETTER EXPLAIN...
SEE, MUZZ, HE DOESN'T TALK CHINESEY!
I AM AFRAID THIS HUMBLE SERVANT OF CHINA HAS DECEIVED YOU!... AS YOU NOTICE, I SPEAK YOUR LANGUAGE QUITE PASSABLY!
MILTON CANIFF
PASSABLY? YOU SOUND LIKE THE VALEDICTORIAN OF THE CLASS OF 1942! ...WHAT'S BUZZIN', COUSIN?
THERE IS MUCH TO EXPLAIN... BUT FIRST, LET ME CAUTION MADAME AGAINST LEANING TOO HEAVILY ON THAT PACKING CASE! IT CONTAINS MUCH TRINITROTOLUENE... A MOST DISAGREABLE SUBSTANCE, KNOWN GENERALLY AS T.N.T.

4-21
Reg. U. S. Pat. Off.; Copyright, 1942, by News Syndicate Co. Inc
NIP-NIP, WHEN YOU TOOK US IN AS REFUGEES YOU SPOKE PIDGIN ENGLISH... NOW YOU BUST LOOSE WITH AN IVY LEAGUE ACCENT— AND A HOUSE FULL OF BOOM DUST! HOW COMES IT?
THIS HUMBLE PERSON WAS AN ENGINEERING STUDENT IN THE UNITED STATES WHEN CHINA WAS INVADED!
LIKE MANY ANOTHER, I RETURNED TO DO WHAT I COULD FOR MY COUNTRY! I WAS PUT TO BLOWING UP BRIDGES AND PROCURING MATERIALS TO ENABLE OTHERS TO DO LIKEWISE!...
IT IS SUCH A MISSION THAT BROUGHT ME HERE— TO A VILLAGE OFFERING SOME ESCAPE FROM JAP BOMBERS... GUERILLAS RAID JAP ROAD CREWS AND BRING THE CAPTURED EXPLOSIVES TO ME...
MILTON CANIFF
A SWELL STUNT—BUT JUST HOW DOES IT AFFECT US?
TOO, TOO DIRECTLY! THE ONLY CHANCE YOU HAVE OF LEAVING THIS EVIL SECTION IS TO RIDE DOWN THE RIVER— THROUGH THE JAPANESE BLOCKADE— PACKED INTO MY BOAT BETWEEN CASES OF DYNAMITE!

4-22
Reg. U. S. Pat. Off. Copyright, 1942, by News Syndicate Co. Inc.
MR. RYAN, THERE IS LITTLE TIME TO DECIDE... WILL YOU AND MADAME AND THE SMALL ONE RIDE WITH ME?
GIVE US A FEW MINUTES TO GAB ABOUT IT, NIP-NIP
WHAT DO YOU SAY, NORMANDIE? SHALL WE MAKE A DASH ON NIP-NIP'S DYNAMITE EXPRESS?... NON-STOP RUN... ESPECIALLY IF A TRACER BULLET HITS THE CARGO!
I KNOW HOW MUCH WORSE IT WOULD BE IF WE STAYED AND WERE CAPTURED...
BUT IN SPITE OF THAT POSSIBILITY, I WOULD NOT RISK MERRILY'S LIFE — EXCEPT FOR THE FACT THAT YOU WILL BE WITH US.... I WOULD FOLLOW YOU THROUGH ANYTHING!
YEOW! NIP-NIP!
FULL STEAM AHEAD!... I JUST GOT CLEARANCE PAPERS FROM A DREAM! ...IT WAS A DECLARATION ABOUT A GOOD OLD-FASHIONED CUSTOM! WE CAN TRAVEL AT NIGHT BY THE LIGHT OF THE TORCH I'M CARRYING!...
MILTON CANIFF

4-23
Reg. U. S. Pat. Off.: Copyright, 1942, by News Syndicate Co. Inc.
WHERE ARE WE GOING, MUZZ?
... NIP-NIP HAS A BOAT... HE IS TAKING YOU AND MR. RYAN AND ME TO THE COAST... WE HOPE!
OH, FUN! WILL WE SEE MY DADDY?
NO, MERRILY, DARLING, WE WON'T SEE HIM FOR A LONG TIME...
THEN MR. RYAN WILL BE MY ALMOST DADDY, HUH, MUZZ?
YES, SWEET... HE'LL BE YOUR 'ALMOST' DADDY... AND I WILL BE ALMOST HAPPY!
MILTON CANIFF
YOU KNOW, MUZZ, I LOVE MY DADDY — AND I ALSO LOVE MR. RYAN! ... IS THAT THE RIGHT THING TO DO?
EXCUSE ME, HONEY — I... I... HAVE SOMETHING IN MY EYE!

4-24
Reg. U. S. Pat. Off.: Copyright, 1942, by News Syndicate Co. Inc.
YOU SEE, MR. RYAN, WHILE OUR GUERILLAS BROUGHT STOLEN EXPLOSIVES, I BUILT THIS FALSE COVERING OF LIGHT MATERIAL OVER A POWER BOAT!
YOU WILL POSE AS A FARMER CARRYING HIS STUFF TO MARKET — THEN TRY TO BREAK THROUGH TO... OR SHOULDN'T I TRY TO GUESS OUR DESTINATION?
MR. RYAN IS A DIPLOMAT... FOR THE MOMENT WE WILL CONCERN OURSELVES WITH NOT BEING CAUGHT!
WHAT IF WE ARE CAUGHT, PAT?
WELL...
...THE JAPS WOULD PRACTICE FLOWER ARRANGEMENT ON US — BUT WE WOULDN'T BE ABLE TO APPRECIATE THE SCENT!
MILTON CANIFF
MEANWHILE...
TO THE BOAT! AGAIN WE BROIL IN THE SUN ON THE ACCURSED RIVER PATROL!
...COUNT YOURSELF FORTUNATE THAT YOU ARE NOT ON A TRANSPORT FLEEING FROM A YANKEE FLYING CASTLE! THEN YOU WOULD FEED A FISH... INSTEAD OF EATING ONE!

4-25
Reg. U. S. Pat. Off.: Copyright, 1942, by News Syndicate Co. Inc.
... READY TO CAST OFF, NIP-NIP! THE DYNAMITE LOCAL IS SAILING!
...IT IS WELL! MADAME AND THE SMALL ONE MUST TRY TO BE COMFORTABLE... WHILE REMAINING BELOW DECKS! DISASTER IS MOST APPROXIMATE!
MILTON CANIFF
MEANWHILE, FAR DOWN THE COAST...
THE COMMANDER PACES TO AND FRO! THE NEED FOR OUR MISSING EXPLOSIVES IS ACUTE!...
INDEED! TIME FLEES AS THE MORNING MIST BEFORE THE SUN!
OBSERVE, MY FRIEND, THE SMOKE ON THE HORIZON, RISES FROM THE FUNNELS OF A CONVOY OF JAPANESE SHIPS — MOVING TO SUPPLY THEIR FAR-FLUNG TROOPS!
THIS IS A BAD THING!
BAD, INDEED!.. THE SUBMARINES OF THE AMERICANS FORCE THE DESPISED ONES TO HUG THE SHORE! IF WE HAD EXPLOSIVES WE COULD SPREAD DEVASTATION!.. IT IS A GAMBLE WHETHER THE DRAGON LADY WILL KISS NIP-NIP — OR KILL HIM FOR THE DELAY!

Reg. U. S. Pat. Off.: Copyright, 1942, by News Syndicate Co. Inc.
TERRY AND THE PIRATES by MILTON CANIFF
NIP-NIP, WHEN YOU TOOK MRS. SANDHURST, MERRILY AND ME INTO YOUR VERY HOSPITABLE HIDING PLACE, WE DIDN'T SUSPECT THAT YOU WERE A TOP-SHELF CHINESE GUERILLA!
MR. RYAN IS TOO KIND!... YOU KNEW I WAS ONLY POSING AS A COUNTRY BOY... THE LITTLE ONE TOLD ME!... WHAT YOU DID NOT KNOW WAS THAT I WAS WORKING TO DISGUISE THIS CAPTURED POWER BOAT AS AN INNOCENT RIVER CRAFT... TO FOOL THE ENEMY!
OKAY... BUT YOU NEEDN'T HAVE WORRIED ABOUT US FEARING TO GO DOWN-RIVER WITH YOU... EVEN THOUGH YOU'RE CARRYING HIGH EXPLOSIVES!
WE'VE BEEN SITTING ON DYNAMITE FOR SO LONG — A LITTLE MORE BOOM DUST CAN'T BOTHER US!... I DON'T SUPPOSE IT'S CRICKET TO ASK WHERE WE'RE GOING...
THAT IS A PROBLEM... I CANNOT TAKE YOU TO MY DESTINATION — BUT THERE IS NO PLACE TO LEAVE YOU!
WE'LL TRY NOT TO EMBARRASS YOU, NIP-NIP! MEANWHILE, IF WE DON'T SLIP PAST THE JAP RIVER PATROLS, WE'LL ALL GO STRAIGHT TO A BLANK WALL — WITH A ONE WAY TICKET...
MY PLAN, AS YOU KNOW, IS VERY SIMPLE... WE HAVE A DEEP DRAFT MOTOR LAUNCH WHICH CONTAINS THE EXPLOSIVES... OVER THAT IS BUILT WHAT APPEARS TO BE A RIVER BOAT...
WE MOVE UNDER SAIL WITH THE CURRENT DURING DAYLIGHT ...LIKE ANY FARMER CARRYING PRODUCE... AT NIGHT WE START THE ENGINE AND RUN THE BLOCKADE! WHEN PATROLS APPEAR, MY THREE YANKEE FRIENDS MUST BURROW FOR SAFETY...
OKAY, NIP-NIP, NOTHING LIKE COZYING UP TO A FEW HUNKS OF DYNAMITE TO WARM THE BLOOD!
GHOSTS OF ALL THINGS ANCESTRAL! ... A PATROL APPROACHES AT THIS VERY MOMENT!
NORMANDIE AND MERRILY HAVE BEEN SLEEPING! I'LL GO BELOW AND TUCK THEM INTO OUR FOX HOLE! GOOD LUCK, NIP-NIP!
WHAT IS IT, PAT?
JAP PATROL! NIP-NIP WILL COVER THE FALSE BOTTOM OF THE RIVER BOAT... WE'LL BE SAFE ENOUGH HERE UNLESS THE SOLDIERS ARE TOO THOROUGH!
...I SPEAK YOUR LANGUAGE, SON OF A TIMID TURTLE! WHAT DO YOU CARRY IN THE FILTHY HEAP OF ROTTING PLANKS?
OH, ILLUSTRIOUS ONE, I CARRY PRODUCE TO HELP FEED THE LIBERATORS OF MY UNWORTHY COUNTRY IN THE CITIES DOWN THE RIVER!
107
DO YOU HANDLE THE CLUMSY SCOW YOURSELF?... HAVE YOU NO PRETTY DAUGHTER TO HELP US WHILE AWAY THE TEDIUM OF THIS ACCURSED PATROL?
ALAS, MY HELPERS HAVE BEEN KILLED OFF... FOOLISHLY ATTEMPTING TO FIGHT AGAINST THE UNBEATABLE HOSTS OF NIPPON!... I MUST CARRY ON ALONE!
SHALL WE LOOT HIS CARGO?
NO! ALLOW THE FOOL TO PASS! THE HIGH COMMAND HAS GIVEN THESE BOATMEN QUOTAS OF SUPPLIES TO BRING IN... IF HE IS SHORT HE WILL REPORT US... THIS WAR IS NO LONGER AMUSING! CAST OFF!
AS THE PATROL BOAT PULLS AWAY, A SOLDIER FLIPS A CIGARETTE INTO THE FLIMSY CRATES ON DECK....

4-27
Reg. U. S. Pat. Off.: Copyright, 1942, by News Syndicate Co. Inc.
CLOSE CALL RIGHT OFF THE BAT, NIP-NIP! I'M GLAD THAT JAP PATROL DIDN'T GET TOO CURIOUS!
NIP-NIP MUST CONFESS TO A MOMENT OR TWO APPROXIMATING STAGE FRIGHT! ...HOW DO MADAME AND THE SMALL ONE TAKE TO THE HIDING PLACE?
IT ISN'T BAD... IF YOU DON'T THINK OF THE DYNAMITE PACKED ALL AROUND!... HEY! DO I SEE SMOKE UP FORWARD?
THAT IS SMOKE! QUICKLY, MR. RYAN, ONE OF THE JAP SOLDIERS MAY HAVE FLIPPED A CIGARETTE INTO THE BALES STOWED ON DECK!
IT'S SMOLDERING... WE COULD DOUSE IT— OR TOSS THE BALE OVER THE SIDE...
WE MUST EXTINGUISH THE FLAME! I PACKED DETONATION CAPS IN THE CENTER OF THAT BALE!
MILTON CANIFF

4-28
Reg. U. S. Pat. Off.: Copyright, 1942, by News Syndicate Co. Inc.
HOW'S IT GOING, NIP-NIP?
THE FIRE IS NO MORE...AND THIS HAPLESS ONE IS NEARLY LIKEWISE! IT IS FORTUNATE THAT YOU WERE AT HAND TO TAKE THE TILLER, MR. RYAN!
THE JAP PATROLS HAVEN'T BEEN TOO CURIOUS... IT'S GETTING DARK...DO YOU THINK NORMANDIE AND MERRILY MIGHT GET A BREATH OF AIR?
QUITE SO! THE PATIENT ONES MUST STIFLE IN THEIR CRAMPED HIDING PLACE!
OH, THANKS FOR THE REPRIEVE, PAT! I FEEL LIKE A BLIND MINE MULE!... DON'T GO NEAR THE RAIL, MERRILY, DEAR!
MILTON CANIFF
AT THIS POINT, A STRING OF BARGES LOOMS OUT OF THE HALF LIGHT...

4-29
Reg. U. S. Pat. Off.: Copyright, 1942, by News Syndicate Co. Inc.
NIP-NIP! STRING OF BARGES! DEAD AHEAD!
OH, PRESENCE OF EVIL! IF WE CRASH, OUR CARGO OF HIGH EXPLOSIVES MAY TERMINATE OUR JOURNEY!
WHAT COUSIN OF A WEARY TREE TOAD GUIDES THAT SMELLY MUD SCOW? YOU NEARLY RAMMED US! COME ALONGSIDE AND BE EXAMINED!
JAPANESE GUARD...! THERE IS NO TIME TO HIDE! DROP TO THE DECK!
I WILL COVER YOU UP!
...THIS USELESS ONE APPROACHES! WILL THE WARRIOR HOLD THE POLE TO STEADY MY FRAIL CRAFT?
MILTON CANIFF

4-30
Reg. U. S. Pat. Off.: Copyright, 1942, by News Syndicate Co. Inc.
SPAWN OF THE SICKLY DRAGON! YOU NEARLY RAMMED ONE OF THE EMPEROR'S BARGES!
...IF THE MILITARY ONE WILL HOLD THE POLE TO STEADY THIS MISERABLE RAFT, THERE WILL BE EXPLANATIONS!
QUICKLY, MR. RYAN, CONCEALMENT IS NO LONGER POSSIBLE! WE START THE ENGINES AND TRUST TO LUCK!
...THE SWINE HAS AN ENGINE IN THAT JUNK! SEND UP DANGER FLARES TO WARN THE RIVER PATROL!
SO! BUT FIRST I WILL GIVE HIM A ROUND OR TWO! ...A SHOT MAY FIND HIS GASOLINE TANKS!
MILTON CANIFF

5-1
Reg. U. S. Pat. Off.: Copyright, 1942, by News Syndicate Co. Inc.
UGH!
PAT! NIP-NIP IS HIT!
TAKE CARE OF HIM, NORMANDIE! IF WE DON'T RUN THIS BLOCKADE WE'LL PLAY THE LEADING ROLES IN A MASS SLAUGHTER!
THOSE FLARES ARE PROBABLY TO WARN THE RIVER PATROLS DOWN-STREAM!... I HAVE AN IDEA, NORMANDIE!...
THE JAPS WILL EXPECT US TO RUN FOR IT WITH OUR ENGINE WIDE OPEN!... THAT STRING OF BARGES WE ALMOST HIT WAS MOVING TOWARD THE MOUTH OF THE RIVER!... I THINK WE'LL PLAY A LITTLE QUIET CABOOSE!
WITH THE ENGINE CUT AND SAIL FURLED, PAT SWINGS THE CAMOUFLAGED LAUNCH INTO LINE WITH THE BARGES... AND DISCOVERS A LONE SENTRY ON THE LAST ONE...
MILTON CANIFF

5-2
Reg. U. S. Pat. Off.: Copyright, 1942, by News Syndicate Co. Inc.
WHY DOESN'T SOMEONE TELL ME ABOUT THESE THINGS? SEARCH-LIGHTS GOING... SHOTS BEING FIRED —AND I SIT IN LONELY IGNORANCE ON THIS LAST FOOLISH BARGE!
YI!
I AM FINALLY BEING NOTICED! THAT RIVER MAN WISHES TO THROW ME A LINE!... PERHAPS HE BRINGS NEWS OF ALL THIS EXCITEMENT!
THE SIGNAL LIGHTS INDICATED THAT A MOTOR BOAT WOULD TRY TO RUN THE BLOCKADE... BUT WE HAVE SEEN NOTHING EXCEPT OUR OWN BARGE TRAIN! STRANGE BUSINESS!
...YOU JUST LIE STILL, LITTLE MAN! UNCLE PAT WILL DROP YOU OFF NEAR SHORE... YOU CAN SWIM IN AND TELL YOUR EMPEROR TO PUT SOME EXTRA SCOTCH TAPE ON THE PAPER HOUSES — HE'S GOING TO HAVE GUESTS — AND THEY'LL BRING THEIR OWN EGGS!
MILTON CANIFF

Reg. U. S. Pat. Off.: Copyright, 1942, by News Syndicate Co. Inc.
TERRY AND THE PIRATES
by MILTON CANIFF
HOLY SMOKE! THAT FIRE WAS HARD ENOUGH TO PUT OUT —THEN NIP-NIP WAS HIT IN OUR LAST TUSSLE WITH THE BROWNIES...
MIST' RYAN! NIP-NIP HURT ...BAD... MUST GET LOAD OF EXPLOSIVES TO... FRIENDS! NOT SUPPOSED TO TAKE YOU... BUT CAN'T DO IT MYSELF... WILL YOU STEER IF NIP-NIP... SHOW COURSE AND RECOGNITION SIGNALS?...
SURE THING, NIP-NIP... AFTER ALL, WE WEREN'T HOPING TO MAKE IT TO SAN FRANCISCO!
THE JAPS KNOW WE'RE LOOSE ALONG THIS COAST... THEY GOT A GOOD LOOK AT US BEFORE DARK... THEY'LL KNOW WHAT TO SEARCH FOR TODAY... WHICH GIVES ME AN IDEA...
MAKE THESE ROPES FAST, NORMANDIE... AND YOU AND MERRILY GET INTO SOMETHING RESEMBLING NATIVE COSTUMES... WE'RE GOING TO CHANGE REGISTRY!
RIGHT, PAT!
LATER

WAVE... BUT DON'T SHOW YOUR FACES!
THOSE FISHERMEN WAVE IN FRIENDLY FASHION... WHICH WOULD PROVE NOTHING... BUT THIS SKETCH OF THE FUGITIVE CRAFT DISTINCTLY SHOWS ONE MAST... AND MENTIONS A SINGLE OCCUPANT ONLY! WE MUST SEARCH ELSEWHERE!
THE PLANE'S MOVING ON, NIP-NIP! HOW ABOUT OUR COURSE?
WHEN... WE ARE DUE EAST OF THE... TWIN SMOKE STACKS, STEER FOR SHORE... AND HOIST TWO RED... LANTERNS!
MASTER! IT IS THE SIGNAL OF THE LONG ABSENT NIP-NIP!
5-3
NIP-NIP, INDEED!... THERE IS ANOTHER ON THAT CRAFT WHO IS OF EVEN GREATER INTEREST TO THE DRAGON LADY!

HOW'S NIP-NIP, NORMANDIE?
I CAN'T DO MUCH MORE THAN EASE HIS PAIN A LITTLE, PAT! HE KEEPS ASKING IF WE HAVE SIGHTED THE TWIN SMOKE STACKS!...
5-4 Reg. U. S. Pat. Off.: Copyright, 1942, by News Syndicate Co. Inc.
YES... AND I HOISTED THE TWO RED LANTERNS, AS NIP-NIP DIRECTED... WE'RE STEERING FOR SHORE. I'LL BE GLAD TO BE RID OF THE DYNAMITE ON BOARD!
—THEN WHAT HAPPENS?
THE KIND OF LUCK WE HAD AGAINST THE RIVER PATROLS CAN'T LAST... WE'LL HAVE TO TRY--- HEY! WE'RE GOING TO HAVE COMPANY!
THAT MAN IN THE BOW APPEARS MUCH TOO INNOCENT FOR COMFORT!
MILTON CANIFF

EUROPEANS!
BUT OF COURSE! DID THE COMMANDER NOT SEE THE PALE SKIN THROUGH THE MECHANICAL SPECTACLE?
LOOKING FOR SOMEONE, BOYS?
5-5 Reg. U. S. Pat. Off.: Copyright, 1942, by News Syndicate Co. Inc.
TWO LANTERNS! ... MUST CARRY EXPLOSIVES TO COMMANDER!
BESTIR! IT IS THE VOICE OF NIP-NIP! THIS IS NO JAPANESE TRICK! OUR EXPLOSIVES ARE AT HAND!
MEANWHILE: ON SHORE
HASTEN, MY COMMANDER! THE LONG-AWAITED CRAFT OF NIP-NIP IS BEING ESCORTED TOWARD THIS PLACE!
...DID I NOT SEE IT THROUGH THE GLASS? ...WHY DO YOU GAPE, FOOL?
THE MASTER MAKES USE OF COSMETICS!
ATTEND YOUR SOLDIERING, AMAZED ONE! THE DRAGON LADY IS ABOUT TO ENGAGE IN A BIT OF DIPLOMATIC PLEASANTRY! WHEN WELCOMING THE REPRESENTATIVE OF A FRIENDLY NATION, IT IS WELL TO WEAR ONE'S MOST IMPRESSIVE UNIFORM!
MILTON CANIFF

THE VESSEL OF NIP-NIP IS AT HAND, MY COMMANDER! NIP-NIP LIES WOUNDED– THE CRAFT WAS GUIDED HERE BY ONE RYAN, AN AMERICAN!
ATTEND NIP-NIP'S WOUNDS...I WILL SEE HIM PRESENTLY... BRING RYAN HERE!
5-6
Reg. U. S. Pat. Off.: Copyright, 1942, by News Syndicate Co. Inc.
THE SOLDIER SAID WE--WHY, IF IT ISN'T THE DRAGON LADY!
MILTON CANIFF

PAT, WHY DOES THAT WOMAN REACT THIS WAY– AFTER WE BROUGHT NIP-NIP AND THE HIGH EXPLOSIVES ALL THE WAY HERE? WHO IS SHE?
SHE'S THE DRAGON LADY... A FORMER PIRATE QUEEN... NOW SHE FIGHTS FOR CHINA! SHE MUST BE THE BOSS OF THIS OUTFIT!
HA HA HA...
5-7
Reg. U. S. Pat. Off.: Copyright, 1942, by News Syndicate Co. Inc.
OF COURSE I AM THE BOSS HERE! ... BUT THE HANDSOME ONE DOES NOT EXPLAIN WHY THE DRAGON LADY LAUGHS!
I KNOW WHY...
SHE THINKS YOU ARE MARRIED TO ME... AND THAT MERRILY IS YOUR CHILD!
IS THIS NOT SO?
NO... MR. RYAN IS JUST AN OLD FRIEND! ...I HAVE NO HOLD ON HIM!... I AM SURE YOU UNDERSTAND WHAT I MEAN!
MILTON CANIFF

HEY, BEAUTIFUL, WHAT KIND OF HOSPITALITY IS THIS? WE HAULED NIP-NIP AND HIS LOAD OF DYNAMITE THROUGH THE JAP PATROLS — AND YOU'RE ABOUT AS GRACIOUS AS A TIGRESS AT FEEDING TIME!
PARDON!... THE DRAGON LADY WAS DISCONCERTED BY THE THOUGHT OF RYAN AS A FATHER!
5-8
Reg. U. S. Pat. Off.: Copyright, 1942, by News Syndicate Co. Inc.
THE WOMAN AND CHILD WILL TAKE SHELTER IN THIS HUT — TEMPORARILY!....THE DRAGON LADY GOES TO SEE NIP-NIP... AFTER WHICH SHE WILL SPEAK WITH RYAN — ALONE!
WELL, PAT, IT'S OBVIOUS THAT YOUR EXOTIC FRIEND IS NOT HAPPY TO HAVE MERRILY AND ME AROUND!
SHE'S RUNNING A FRONT-LINE FIGHTING UNIT HERE, NORMANDIE! —THAT'S WHY A WOMAN AND CHILD SEEM OUT OF PLACE...
MILTON CANIFF
SHE AND I HAVE BEEN THROUGH SO MANY THINGS TOGETHER—SHE FIGURES I MIGHT COME IN HANDY!
...THE LAST REASON IS THE ONE I HAD IN MIND!

NICE LITTLE LAYOUT YOU'VE GOT HERE, BEAUTIFUL! HOW'S NIP-NIP?
OUR SURGEON IS AT WORK... HE WILL BE WELL SOON ENOUGH! HE TOLD ME OF YOUR ADVENTURE!...
5-9
Reg. U. S. Pat. Off.: Copyright, 1942, by News Syndicate Co. Inc.
IF I HAD KNOWN THOSE EXPLOSIVES WERE FOR YOU I WOULD HAVE RUSHED THEM HERE MUCH SOONER!
THE GLIB TONGUE RETAINS ITS SHARP EDGE ... IT IS ESPECIALLY NOTICEABLE SINCE ITS OWNER KNOWS THE DRAGON LADY IS NOW UNDER OBLIGATION TO HIM!
WHAT KIND OF TALK IS THAT?.. WE'RE ALLIES NOW, BABE! I'LL BE GLAD TO HELP YOU PLANT THAT WHAM-STUFF UNDER SOME OF THE LITTLE FLOWER-ARRANGERS!
... I AM AWARE OF THE HANDSOME ONE'S ABILITIES —I AM FURTHER AWARE OF HIS SHREWDNESS AS A BARGAINER! IN RETURN FOR HIS GOOD EFFORTS, THE DRAGON LADY MUST OFFER SHELTER TO THE MOUSEY ONE AND HER CHILD! IT IS THE FIRST TIME I EVER HAD TO BECOME A SOCIAL WORKER IN ORDER TO HOLD A MAN!
MILTON CANIFF

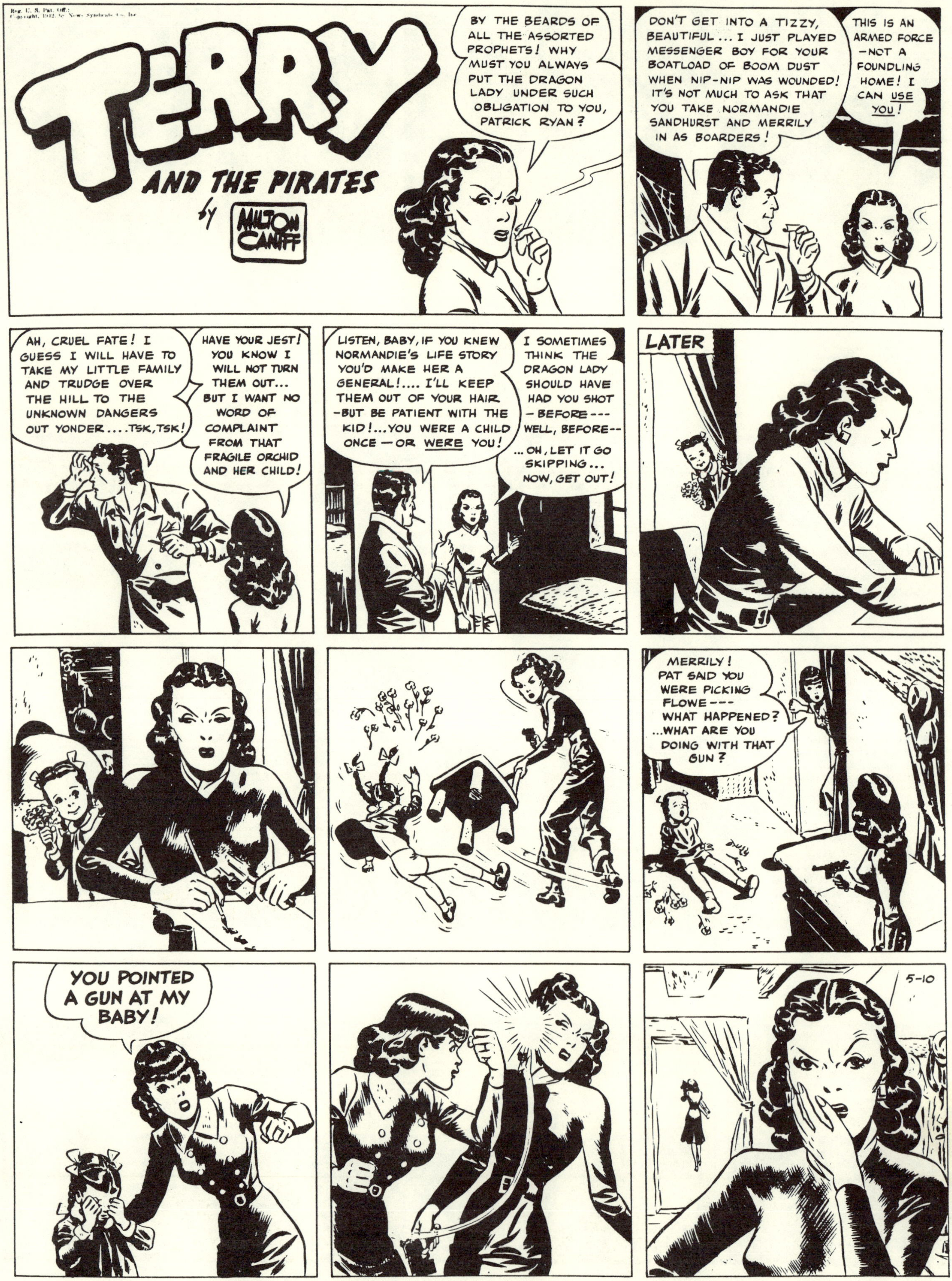

WHAT'S THE MATTER, NORMANDIE?... ONE WOULDN'T THINK TO LOOK AT YOU THAT WE HAD BROUGHT A MESS OF DYNAMITE THROUGH THE JAP. LINES WITHOUT STARTING A PREMATURE 4TH OF JULY CELEBRATION!
IT ISN'T THAT, PAT... I HAVE JUST ACTED LIKE A GUTTERSNIPE! ...I HIT YOUR FRIEND, THE DRAGON LADY, WITH MY FIST!
HUH?
MERRILY PICKED SOME FLOWERS AND TOOK THEM TO THE DRAGON LADY... THE BABY MUST HAVE STARTLED HER— WHEN I LOOKED IN, THE WOMAN WAS HOLDING A GUN ON MERRILY... WHO WAS SCREAMING!... I STRUCK THE DRAGON LADY IN THE FACE... AND WALKED OUT!
HMMM!... YOU SEEM TO BE HEALTHY— AND ALL IN ONE PIECE!... —BUT WHAT A LITTLE SPENDTHRIFT YOU ARE!
WHAT DO YOU MEAN, PAT?
YOU'VE USED UP YOUR NORMAL RATION OF LUCK WITH ONE PUNCH! HOW WILL YOU GET THROUGH THE REMAINDER OF THE WAR?
MILTON CANIFF
5-11
Reg. U. S. Pat. Off. Copyright, 1942, by News Syndicate Co. Inc.

ARE YOU SLIPPING, BEAUTIFUL? NORMANDIE TELLS ME SHE SOCKED YOU FOR POINTING A GUN AT LITTLE MERRILY —AND YOU DIDN'T CUT OFF EVEN ONE OF HER EARS!
THE DRAGON LADY HAS ALWAYS BEEN SELFISH... AS YOU HAVE REMINDED ME BEFORE, RYAN... BUT THIS WAR HAS BROUGHT A NEW SET OF VALUES!
I KNOW WHY THE QUIET MOUSE SUDDENLY BECAME A LIONESS WHEN SHE THOUGHT HER BABY WAS THREATENED... THE MEN IN MY COMMAND MUST OBEY ME WITHOUT QUESTION —AS A CHILD OBEYS ITS PARENTS... I WOULD STAND ALONE AGAINST ANY ODDS TO PROTECT THEM...
FOR THIS DEVOTION, I PROVIDE THEM WITH DIVERSION WHEN THEY ARE NOT CALLED UPON TO OFFER THEIR LIVES..... THE PEOPLE OF CHINA ARE TOO POOR TO GIVE MONEY FOR SUCH PURPOSES — AS DO THE CITIZENS OF YOUR COUNTRY ...MEN FIGHT BETTER WHEN THEY KNOW THEY WILL FIND RELAXATION BETWEEN BATTLES...
THE DRAGON LADY HAS BECOME AWARE OF THESE THINGS... IT IS UNDERSTOOD. THEN, WHY THE CULTURED NORMANDIE STRUCK AS A WILD ANIMAL PROTECTING HER YOUNG..
EASY DOES IT, BEAUTIFUL... BELIEVE ME, YOU LOOK VERY WELL WITH YOUR HAIR DOWN!
... BUT RYAN IS NOT TO CONCLUDE FROM ALL THIS THAT THE DRAGON LADY HAS GONE SOFT---
MILTON CANIFF
5-12
Reg. U. S. Pat. Off.: Copyright, 1942, by News Syndicate Co. Inc.

WELL, BEAUTIFUL, I'M RELIEVED THAT YOU AREN'T ANGRY WITH NORMANDIE AND MERRILY! TELL ME ABOUT YOUR SETUP HERE...
THE JAPANESE SUPPLY SHIPS MOVE SOUTHWARD IN A CONSTANT STREAM... OUR TASK IS TO WAIT UNTIL YOUR AMERICAN SUBMARINES FORCE THEM TOWARD SHORE —THEN WE STRIKE!
THAT'S A BIG ORDER... HAVEN'T THE JAPS SPOTTED YOU HERE?
WE KEEP MOVING ABOUT! OF COURSE THE ENEMY ATTEMPTS TO LOCATE OUR BASES-BUT MR. TOJO IS VERY BUSY THESE DAYS... HE SPREADS HIS STRENGTH THINLY!
WILL THIS INTRUSION BE FORGIVEN BY MY COMMANDER?..OUR PATROL PICKED UP A MAN FLOATING ON A BIT OF WRECKAGE! WILL YOU SEE HIM?
YOU KNOW I SEE ANY STRANGER WHO ENTERS THIS AREA! BRING HIM HERE!
IF THE RESCUED ONE IS CHINESE, LET HIM SPEAK IN THAT LANGUAGE!
OH, NOBLE COMMANDER, A FORTUNATE PERSON STANDS BEFORE YOU... I WAS ONE OF THE CREW OF A FISHING VESSEL SHELLED BY THE ACCURSED JAPANESE!... THE WAR BOAT SOUGHT A FUGITIVE JUNK SIMILAR TO OURS! ENRAGED BY THEIR ERROR, THEY SANK OUR BOAT—I AM THE LONE SURVIVOR!
MILTON CANIFF
5-13
Reg. U. S. Pat. Off.: Copyright, 1942, by News Syndicate Co. Inc.

...HE SAYS HIS JUNK WAS MISTAKEN FOR A FUGITIVE AND SUNK... THE JAPS ARE STILL LOOKING FOR YOU AND THE EXPLOSIVES, RYAN!
SO YOUR CREW WAS LOST... WHY ARE YOU NOT.... IN THE CHINESE ARMY?
... BUT I WORKED FOR MY COUNTRY, OH NOBLE COMMANDER!
THE MAN HAS BEEN SEARCHED!... NO WEAPONS!
MY CREW LABORED AS FISHERMEN BY LIGHT OF DAY —AT NIGHT WE SMUGGLED MUCH WAR MATERIAL THROUGH THE JAPANESE COASTAL PATROLS!
WHAT LITTLE HE TELLS OF HIS WORK SOUNDS AUTHENTIC —AND HE SPEAKS THE COMMON DIALECT WITH EASE...
—BUT WE TAKE NO CHANCES... THE JAPANESE ARE CLEVER AT PLANTING SPIES BY SUCH METHODS! WE WILL TEST HIM!
REMOVE HIS SLIPPERS!
HIS FEET ARE WELL FORMED! HE DOES NOT HAVE THE WIDE SPACE BETWEEN THE FIRST AND SECOND TOES USUALLY FOUND IN THE JAPANESE PEASANT GROUP...
YEP... HE'S WORN SHOES AND NOT SANDALS MOST OF HIS LIFE... —WHICH MIGHT BE TRUE OF ONE OF THE OFFICER CLASS... YOU'LL HAVE TO TRY AGAIN, BEAUTIFUL!
MILTON CANIFF
5-14
Reg. U. S. Pat. Off. Copyright, 1942, by News Syndicate Co. Inc.

IF THIS MAN OUR PATROL PICKED UP ON SOME FLOATING WRECKAGE IS A JAPANESE SPY, HE IS A CLEVER ONE...
HIS FEET ARE NOT MARKED BY THE USUAL JAPANESE SANDAL CALLOUS BETWEEN THE FIRST AND SECOND TOES... WHY NOT TRY THE ENGLISH PRONUNCIATION TEST ON HIM!
5-15
Reg. U. S. Pat. Off.: Copyright, 1942, by News Syndicate Co. Inc.
YOU ARE, OF COURSE, UNDER SUSPICION AS A SPY... YOU WILL REPEAT AFTER ME THE FOLLOWING SENTENCE IN THE ENGLISH TONGUE...
IT IS RISKY TO FOLLOW THE HORSES...
THE ENGLISH SPEECH IS UNKNOWN TO ME — BUT I WILL ATTEMPT TO REPEAT...
"IT IS LISKY TO FOLLOW THE HOLSES"
THAT IS THE WAY A CHINESE WOULD SPEAK! IF HE WERE JAPANESE HE WOULD HAVE SAID... "IT IS-S-S-S RIS-S-SKY TO FORROW THE HORS-S-SES-S-S"
RIGHT... IF HE IS A SPY — HE'S A SMOOTHIE... HIS TEETH ARE NOT SO BUCKY — AND HIS NOSE IS STRAIGHT...
MILTON CANIFF
THE STRANGER SEEMS TO BE ALL THAT HE CLAIMS — BUT HE WILL BE PUT IN QUARANTINE UNTIL IT IS EVIDENT THAT HE POSSESSES NO CONTAGIOUS DISEASE...
THE NOBLE COMMANDER IS MOST GRACIOUS... THIS HUMBLE PERSON IS THANKFUL FOR SUCH HOSPITALITY...

THE FISHERMAN YOUR PATROL PICKED UP HAS BEEN IN YOUR QUARANTINE CHAMBER FOR 24 HOURS, BEAUTIFUL... HAVE YOU DECIDED TO ACCEPT HIM AS CHINESE?
BY NO MEANS, RYAN... DURING THE NIGHT THE ROOM WAS HEATED TO A SWELTERING TEMPERATURE...
5-16
Reg. U. S. Pat. Off.: Copyright, 1942, by News Syndicate Co. Inc.
WE WILL SEE WHAT OUR MAN LOOKS LIKE AFTER SO MANY HOURS OF OPEN PORES...
THE CHINESE IS GENERALLY SMOOTH-FACED... THE JAPANESE HAS A HEAVY BEARD... THIS MAN PROBABLY SHAVED JUST BEFORE WE PICKED HIM UP — AND INTENDED TO DO SO IN SECRET AFTER HE JOINED US... BUT HE WILL NOT HAVE THE CHANCE... TAKE HIM AWAY!
MILTON CANIFF

TERRY AND THE PIRATES
by MILTON CANIFF
I TOLD YOU NORMANDIE HAD COURAGE! WHO ELSE EVER SOCKED THE DRAGON LADY AND LIVED?
AFTER ALL THESE YEARS OF WAR WITH JAPAN, WE IN CHINA UNDERSTAND STRIKING AGAINST ANY ODDS TO PROTECT WHAT WE LOVE!... WHAT HAS HAPPENED TO CREATE THIS GREAT BOND BETWEEN THE LITTLE NORMANDIE AND THE DASHING RYAN?
WHEN TERRY AND I LANDED IN CHINA YEARS AGO...
"...I GOT A JOB AS SECRETARY TO CHAUNCEY DRAKE, THE BIG SHIPPING MAN. HIS NIECE, NORMANDIE DRAKE, WAS A SNIPPITY KID — WITH MORE MONEY THAN MANNERS...
"HOWEVER, WHEN THE CHIPS WERE DOWN, THIS KID PROVED HERSELF BIG LEAGUE ALL THE WAY. I REALIZED THAT NORMANDIE WAS GOOD FOR ME — EVEN IF I WASN'T GOOD FOR HER...
"JUST BEFORE THE MAIN EVENT, HER AUNT POPPED UP AND WHISKED HER OFF TO THE UNITED STATES TO SAVE HER DARLING FROM 'THAT AWFUL ADVENTURER'...

"NORMANDIE, BEING AN ORPHAN, WAS INDEBTED TO HER AUNT AND UNCLE — SO SHE MARRIED THE MAN HER AUNT HAD HOOKED... HE WAS TONY SANDHURST... VERY PROPER BACKGROUND BUT MISSING A BEAT IN THE BACKBONE...."

"...THE NEXT TIME I SAW NORMANDIE SHE WAS STICKING LOYALLY TO THIS DOPE — WHO DID EVERYTHING IN THE BAD BOOK BUT BEAT HER IN PUBLIC! HE GOT IN A BUSINESS JAM — AND TRIED TO PIN THE THING ON ME..."

"...THE POOR KID WAS ABOUT TO HAVE A BABY — BUT SHE BROKE OUT OF THE HOUSE WHERE SANDHURST HAD LOCKED HER, IN ORDER TO TESTIFY IN COURT ON MY BEHALF... I WAS FREED — THE HUSBAND DISAPPEARED"

"WHILE SHE WAS IN THE HOSPITAL, AN OLD GOAT NAMED CAPTAIN JUDAS SNATCHED TERRY AND ME — AND I DIDN'T SEE HER AND THE BABY UNTIL THE WAR STARTED... BY THAT TIME HER HUSBAND HAD TURNED UP AGAIN... THIS TIME WORKING FOR THE JAPS...."

"...NORMANDIE REMAINED LOYAL TO THIS CLUNK, IN SPITE OF EVERYTHING — I HAD TO HANG ONE ON HIM TO KEEP HIM FROM SACRIFICING HIS WIFE AND CHILD TO SAVE HIS OWN HIDE... YOU KNOW THE REST...."

"THE DRAGON LADY IS MORE AMUSED THAN IMPRESSED BY THAT PROSAIC RECITAL!... IT IS MOST CONVENIENT FOR THE HANDSOME BACHELOR TO CARRY THE SO-CALLED 'TORCH' FOR THE SAFELY MARRIED WOMAN.... THE FOOTLOOSE RYAN IS STILL HAPPILY DISTANT FROM THE FIRESIDE AND CARPET SLIPPERS!"

"YOU SENT FOR ME, MISS DRAGON LADY!"

"I DID, MADAME SANDHURST! YOU KNOW, OF COURSE, THAT I COULD HAVE HAD YOU AND YOUR CHILD SHOT FOR THE INCIDENT INVOLVING YOUR STRIKING THE COMMANDING OFFICER OF THIS MILITARY POST..."

"YES, I UNDERSTAND..."

"PATRICK RYAN TOLD ME SOMETHING OF YOUR BACKGROUND... IT IS OBVIOUS THAT YOU HAVE A HOLD ON HIM... HE IS IN LOVE WITH YOU! IS THIS NOT TRUE?"

"SO HE SAYS..."

"THE DRAGON LADY NEEDS RYAN'S SKILL IN A MILITARY RAID... HE MAY HESITATE TO JOIN ME — FOR FEAR OF LEAVING YOU AND THE CHILD UNPROTECTED..."

"...I WOULD LIKE YOUR PROMISE THAT YOU WILL NOT TRY TO KEEP RYAN FROM JOINING FORCES WITH ME IN A RAID ON JAPANESE SHIPPING!"

"NOW THAT YOU HAVE USED THE PRESSURE OF MY STRIKING YOU TO FORCE ME TO AGREE... WHY DON'T YOU ADMIT WHY YOU REALLY WANT ME TO KEEP QUIET?"

"YOU'RE USING THE FACT THAT I STRUCK YOU TO KEEP ME FROM DETAINING PAT RYAN WHEN YOU ASK HIM TO HELP YOU RAID JAPANESE SHIPPING... WHY NOT COME RIGHT OUT WITH THE ACTUAL REASON YOU WISH TO SILENCE ME?"

"HMMM... RYAN SAID YOU HAD COURAGE... YOU ARE EVIDENTLY FOOLHARDY AS WELL!... WHY DOES THE LITTLE MOUSE THINK THERE IS ANOTHER REASON?"

"YOU CAN PROBABLY DECEIVE MOST MEN — EVEN PAT... INTO THINKING YOU HAVE NO HUMAN SENSIBILITIES... BUT IT IS PERFECTLY CLEAR TO A WOMAN THAT YOU ARE IN LOVE WITH HIM!..."

"YOU... I'LL—"

"I CAN HARDLY STOP YOU FROM HURTING ME... BUT I DON'T KNOW WHY YOU SHOULD BE SO INCENSED! I HAVE NO HOLD ON PAT... YOU HAVE A PERFECT RIGHT TO BE IN LOVE WITH HIM — IF YOU WISH..."

"YOU ARE A STRANGE CREATURE... YOU MAKE NO CLAIM ON RYAN... ALTHOUGH HE SAYS HE LOVES YOU... IS IT BECAUSE OF YOUR HUSBAND — WHO EVEN YOU ADMIT HAS TREATED YOU BADLY?"

"PERHAPS THE ALL-POWERFUL DRAGON LADY AND THE STRANGE MOUSE ARE MORE ALIKE THAN YOU WOULD CARE TO THINK... PLEASE DON'T HAVE ME SHOT IF I TELL YOU WHY..."

WHAT DOES MADAME SANDHURST MEAN BY SAYING SHE AND THE DRAGON LADY ARE ALIKE?
YOU SAY PAT RYAN IS IN LOVE WITH ME— AND YOU ARE SURPRISED THAT I DO NOT FLY TO HIS ARMS... FRANKLY, I WAS JUST AS SURPRISED WHEN YOU DID NOT DO AWAY WITH ME AS SOON AS WE ARRIVED HERE... —SO THAT YOU COULD HAVE HIM!...
5-20
Reg. U. S. Pat. Off.: Copyright, 1942, by News Syndicate Co. Inc.
...I COULD NOT DENY...TO ANOTHER WOMAN... THAT I WOULD ENJOY THE LUXURY OF BEING ADORED BY PAT... BUT IF I DID NOT KEEP THE BARGAIN I MADE WITH MY HUSBAND, I WOULD NOT BE TRUE TO MYSELF!... MY PERSONAL INTEGRITY IS ALL I HAVE IN THE WORLD BESIDES LITTLE MERRILY...
GO ON!
I HAVE HEARD HOW CRUEL YOU ARE TO YOUR ENEMIES —BUT THAT YOU ALWAYS KEEP A BARGAIN—NO MATTER HOW DISTASTEFUL... TO MAINTAIN YOUR PERSONAL STANDARDS...WHETHER THEY ARE RIGHT OR WRONG IS NOT FOR ME TO JUDGE... YOU HAVE SET YOURSELF AGAINST THE WORLD... FALLING IN LOVE HAS NO PLACE IN YOUR CODE...
... ANALYSIS FROM SUCH A LITTLE ONE IS MOST SURPRISING... BUT YOU SAID BEFORE THAT THE DRAGON LADY WANTED YOU OUT OF THE WAY- TO HAVE A CLEAR FIELD WITH RYAN...
YOU ARE HUMAN—EVEN THOUGH FEW PEOPLE WOULD BELIEVE IT...YOU MIGHT NEVER THROW YOURSELF AT HIS FEET —BUT YOU WANT TO BE CERTAIN NO OTHER WOMAN IS AROUND TO LURE HIM AWAY WHILE YOU MAKE UP YOUR MIND...YOU ARE A PROFESSIONAL GAMBLER... ONLY BETTING ON SURE THINGS!
MILTON CANIFF

... THE WEAPON OF THIS THOUGHTLESS SOLDIER IS FOULED WITH DIRT! SUCH CARELESSNESS ON A RAID AGAINST THE JAPANESE MAY COST PRECIOUS LIVES! THE SOLDIER WILL RECEIVE THE USUAL PUNISHMENT!
5-21
Reg. U. S. Pat. Off.: Copyright, 1942, by News Syndicate Co. Inc.
?
AND WHAT DOES THE GRINNING ONE FIND SO AMUSING ABOUT ALL THIS?
THE ANSWER LIES IN THE REAR!
MILTON CANIFF

... THE GIRL-CHILD APED THE COMMANDING ONE! THERE WILL BE DIRE CONSEQUENCES!
GO INSIDE THE HUT, TINY ONE!
IT IS FRIGHTFUL TO CONTEMPLATE!
5-22
Reg. U. S. Pat. Off.: Copyright, 1942, by News Syndicate Co. Inc.
DID I DO SOMETHING WRONG, MISS DRAGON LADY?
RULES MUST EXIST BEFORE THEY MAY BE BROKEN!... ONE DOUBTS IF THE SMALL CHILD HAS EVER BEEN TOLD NOT TO IMITATE MILITARY LEADERS AT AN INSPECTION OF TROOPS... HOWEVER, TO ADULTS IT IS A SERIOUS THING...
OWR! OW! OH! OUCH!
IT IS AS ONE EXPECTED! THE WRATH OF THE COMMANDER DESCENDS EVEN UPON THE PERSON OF THE HELPLESS GIRL-CHILD!
OW! OH!
...THAT WILL BE ENOUGH TO CREATE THE PROPER IMPRESSION! RUN ALONG TO YOUR MOTHER... BUT DO NOT DARE TELL ANYONE OF OUR LITTLE GAME... IT TOOK MANY YEARS TO BUILD UP THE DRAGON LADY'S REPUTATION!
MILTON CANIFF

... NORMANDIE! THE DRAGON LADY'S SPIES JUST REPORTED A JAP CONVOY FORMING TO RUN CLOSE TO SHORE TO AVOID A FLOCK OF OUR SUBS!
OH!
5-23
Reg. U. S. Pat. Off.: Copyright, 1942, by News Syndicate Co. Inc.
THE DRAGON LADY PICKED THIS OUTFIT AND TRAINED THE MEN TO ATTACK SHIPS FROM THE SURFACE! IT WILL MEAN A BLOW AT THE JAPS AND SOME MUCH-NEEDED WAR MATERIAL—IF IT WORKS—
I KNOW, PAT!
I THINK THE DRAGON LADY HAD AN IDEA YOU AND MERRILY WOULD BE FRIGHTENED TO STAY HERE WHILE I AM AWAY ON THIS RAID! SHE DIDN'T KNOW THE KIND OF STUFF YOU'RE MADE OF! I'M OFF TO TALK OVER THE PLANS... SEE YOU LATER...
S-SO LONG!
MILTON CANIFF
MUZZ, WHY IS THERE BLOOD ON YOUR LOWER LIP?

Reg. U. S. Pat. Off.
News Syndicate Co. Inc.
TERRY AND THE PIRATES by MILTON CANIFF
THE TIME HAS COME FOR THE CAPABLE RYAN TO ASSIST 'THE' DRAGON LADY IN MAKING LIFE MOST UNPLEASANT FOR THE MEN WHO CARRY SUPPLIES TO THE ARMIES OF NIPPON!
YOUR EARLY TRAINING AS A PIRATE MUST BE A BIG HELP JUST NOW, BEAUTIFUL!
THE DRAGON LADY'S PAST IS NOT THE SUBJECT UNDER DISCUSSION! THE FLIPPANT RYAN WILL DO WELL TO PAY CAREFUL ATTENTION!
MOST OF OUR EQUIPMENT WAS TAKEN FROM ENEMY CASUALTIES...THE ONLY JAPS WHO ARE WELCOME TO A PERMANENT PLACE ON CHINESE SOIL!...WE PAINT THE HELMETS, METAL AND LEATHER BLACK, WEAR BLACK CLOTHES—AND SMEAR OUR HANDS AND FACES WITH GREASE!
JUST AN OLD-TIME MINSTREL SHOW—WITH GAGS RESERVED FOR SENTRIES!
WHEN YOU MET NIP-NIP HE WAS COLLECTING EXPLOSIVES, STOLEN FROM JAPANESE POSTS BY OUR GUERILLAS! FROM THEM WE FASHION MINES, GRENADES AND TORPEDOES!...
...AND EVEN IF YOU CAUSE ONLY SLIGHT DAMAGE, YOU FORCE THE JAPS TO DIVERT AIRCRAFT TO PROTECT THEIR CONVOYS ON EVERY TRIP!
EXACTLY! YOUR AMERICAN SUBMARINES FORCE JAP SHIPS TO HUG THE SHORE... WE TAKE THEM IN THE NARROW PLACES BETWEEN THE ISLANDS!... PLEASE PREPARE YOURSELF... WE HAVE NEWS OF A CONVOY!
...OKAY, BEAUTIFUL! ♫ WHEN I SAL-LY FORTH TO MEET MY PREY...I HELP MY-SELF IN A ROY-AL WAY...♫
THERE ARE BUT TWO COPIES OF THE MAP WE WILL USE! THE LEGENDS ON YOURS ARE IN ENGLISH!
THAT'S GOOD! I DON'T WANT TO END UP IN TIBET!
MUZZ WENT TO GET OUR FOOD! WHAT'S THAT, MR. RYAN?
THINGS I'M TAKING ON A LITTLE HUNTING TRIP, MERRILY!... I'LL GO HELP YOUR MOTHER!
LATER...
COME ALONG MERRILY!... DINNER WILL BE COLD!
... I'LL SEE YOU BEFORE WE LEAVE, NORMANDIE! I HAVE TO STUDY OUR ROUTE!
5-24
Important Landmarks in RED
Jap Supply Depot
Diversion here
Jap Plane Spotter
Bombers & Fighters
Diversion here
Airport
High cliff
Terminus of R.R.
Convoy Route
Diversion party
Hull of Sunken Ship
Rendezvous here
Raid here
Jap Patrol
Scale
15 Miles
Retreat
Alternate Retreat

HAUL THE FLATBOATS FROM THEIR HIDING PLACES IN THE VALLEY! WE MUST BE READY TO MOVE JUST AFTER DARK!
ANY NEWS OF THE JAP CONVOY, BEAUTIFUL?
5-25
Reg. U. S. Pat. Off.: Copyright, 1942, by News Syndicate Co. Inc
YES, RYAN, IT MOVES SOUTH — CLOSE TO SHORE! WE SHALL STRIKE AT ONE SHIP — AT A POINT WHERE WE KNOW THE WATER TO BE SHALLOW!
DO YOU THINK WE CAN SALVAGE ENOUGH WAR MATERIAL BEFORE THE ESCORT COUNTER-ATTACKS?
EVERY MAN WILL TAKE PART — ONLY THE WOMEN WILL STAND GUARD HERE! IS LITTLE MADAME SANDHURST RESIGNED TO YOUR TAKING PART IN THIS?
YOU FLATTER ME, BEAUTIFUL! IF NORMANDIE GAVE A HOOT ABOUT ME — SHE WOULD HAVE SHOWN IT BEFORE THIS!
MILTON CANIFF

THE JAPANESE CONVOY WE ARE TO ATTACK WILL HAVE PATROL PLANES AND POSSIBLY BLIMPS! OUR CRAFT WILL MOVE CLOSE TO LAND — SO THE WAKES WILL BLEND WITH THE SHORE LINE IN THE POOR LIGHT! ARE YOU READY, RYAN?
HAVE TO PUT THE MAKEUP ON STRAIGHT! IF WE DO A GOOD SHOW WE MAY GET A BROADWAY TRYOUT!
5-26
Reg. U. S. Pat. Off.: Copyright, 1942, by News Syndicate Co. Inc.
NORMANDIE, COULD YOU SEE YOUR WAY CLEAR TO KISSING A FELLER GOODBYE BEFORE HE LEAVES FOR THE WARS?
OH, PAT, OF COURSE!
MILTON CANIFF

AW... I'M SORRY, NORMANDIE... I FORGOT THE FACE PAINT FOR THE RAID ON THE CONVOY! THAT GOODBYE KISS SORT OF RUBBED OFF ON YOU!
THAT'S ALL RIGHT, PAT!... SO LONG! GOOD LUCK!
5-27
Reg. U. S. Pat. Off.: Copyright, 1942, by News Syndicate Co. Inc.
GROWNUPS ARE FUNNY... IF MY FACE WAS DIRTY I WOULD HAVE HAD TO WASH IT A LONG TIME AGO!
MILTON CANIFF

WE MUST BE NEARING THE SPOT WHERE YOU PLAN TO INTERCEPT THE JAP CONVOY, BEAUTIFUL! ARE YOU SURE OF YOUR TIMING!
THE CAUTIOUS RYAN DOES NOT REALIZE HOW ADEPT THE CHINESE HAVE BECOME OVER THE YEARS OF FIGHTING WITH SO FEW WEAPONS!
5-28
THE JAPANESE MUST USE COOLIE LABOR TO LOAD SHIPS AT SHANGHAI AND OTHER CAPTURED PORTS... WE HAVE OUR SPIES AMONG THE LABOR GANGS — AND OUR WARNING SYSTEM SELDOM FAILS!.. WHEN THE CONVOY STEAMS SOUTH WE KNOW WHERE IT WILL BE AT A GIVEN TIME... WE WILL THROW DYNAMITE JUNKS ACROSS ITS PATH AT A GIVEN POINT...
WE HAVE AN AIRPLANE SOUND EFFECT RECORD SALVAGED FROM A HONG KONG RADIO STATION!.. PLAYED OVER A LOUD-SPEAKER, IT WILL CAUSE THE JAPS TO THINK IT IS A NIGHT PLANE ATTACK! AS THEY ACT TO REPEL AERIAL ASSAULT, WE MOVE IN — ON THE SURFACE!
DO YOU THINK NORMANDIE AND MERRILY WILL BE SAFE BACK AT YOUR LAND BASE?
THE DRAGON LADY HAS TAKEN EVERY POSSIBLE PRECAUTION TO PROTECT THE HELPLESS ONES AT THE REAR! IRONICALLY, YOUR PRECIOUS MOUSE AND HER CHILD WILL BENEFIT THEREBY!
MILTON CANIFF

RYAN!
...YES, BEAUTIFUL!
5-29
Reg. U. S. Pat. Off. Copyright, 1942, by News Syndicate Co. Inc.
YOU ASKED THE RETICENT MADAME SANDHURST TO KISS YOU GOODBYE ON THE EVE OF BATTLE!
...YES, BEAUTIFUL!
SINCE THE POSSIBILITY OF DEATH IS ALWAYS PRESENT ON SUCH A RAID AS THIS — I HAVE BEEN THINKING THAT SUCH A CARESS HAS A VERY LASTING QUALITY!... SO I WOULD LIKE TO ASK A FAVOR OF YOU...
WHY, BEAUTIFUL, ...THIS IS SO SUDDEN...WHAT IN THE WORLD COULD YOU BE WANTING?
I WOULD LIKE YOU TO REMEMBER THAT YOU ARE UNDER MY COMMAND — AND IF IT BECOMES NECESSARY TO ABANDON THOSE WOMEN AT THE BASE, IN ORDER TO RETREAT IN ANOTHER DIRECTION, THAT YOU WILL NOT MAKE SOME FOOLISHLY HEROIC GESTURE TO RESCUE THEM — WITH THE RESULT THAT THE DRAGON LADY WILL HAVE TO ORDER YOU SHOT!
MILTON CANIFF

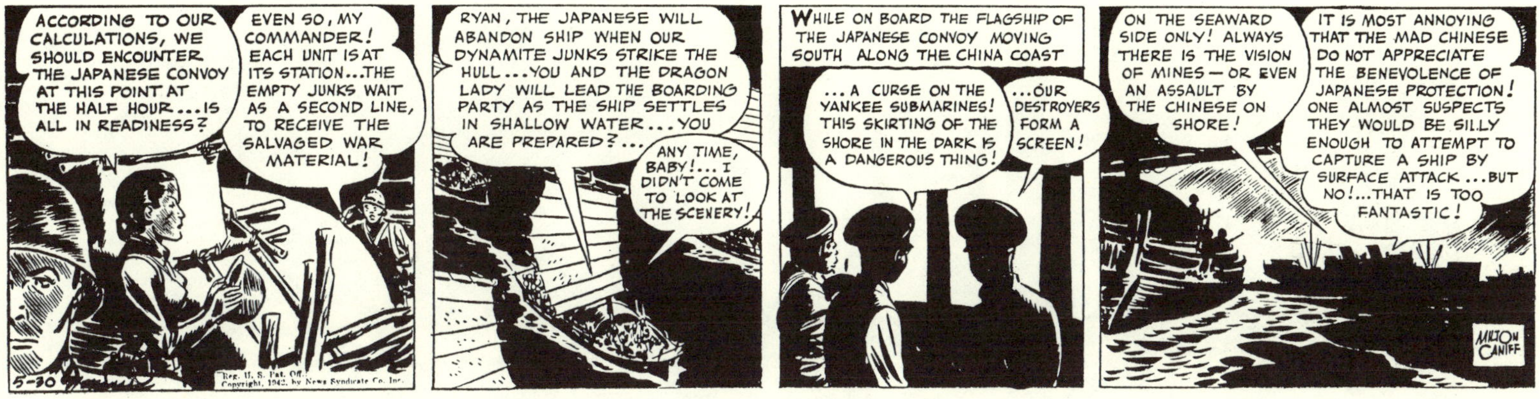
ACCORDING TO OUR CALCULATIONS, WE SHOULD ENCOUNTER THE JAPANESE CONVOY AT THIS POINT AT THE HALF HOUR...IS ALL IN READINESS?
EVEN SO, MY COMMANDER! EACH UNIT IS AT ITS STATION...THE EMPTY JUNKS WAIT AS A SECOND LINE, TO RECEIVE THE SALVAGED WAR MATERIAL!
5-30
Reg. U. S. Pat. Off. Copyright, 1942, by News Syndicate Co. Inc.
RYAN, THE JAPANESE WILL ABANDON SHIP WHEN OUR DYNAMITE JUNKS STRIKE THE HULL...YOU AND THE DRAGON LADY WILL LEAD THE BOARDING PARTY AS THE SHIP SETTLES IN SHALLOW WATER...YOU ARE PREPARED?...
ANY TIME, BABY!... I DIDN'T COME TO LOOK AT THE SCENERY!
WHILE ON BOARD THE FLAGSHIP OF THE JAPANESE CONVOY MOVING SOUTH ALONG THE CHINA COAST
...A CURSE ON THE YANKEE SUBMARINES! THIS SKIRTING OF THE SHORE IN THE DARK IS A DANGEROUS THING!
...OUR DESTROYERS FORM A SCREEN!
ON THE SEAWARD SIDE ONLY! ALWAYS THERE IS THE VISION OF MINES — OR EVEN AN ASSAULT BY THE CHINESE ON SHORE!
IT IS MOST ANNOYING THAT THE MAD CHINESE DO NOT APPRECIATE THE BENEVOLENCE OF JAPANESE PROTECTION! ONE ALMOST SUSPECTS THEY WOULD BE SILLY ENOUGH TO ATTEMPT TO CAPTURE A SHIP BY SURFACE ATTACK...BUT NO!...THAT IS TOO FANTASTIC!
MILTON CANIFF

Reg. U. S. Pat. Off. Copyright, 1942, by News Syndicate Co. Inc.
TERRY AND THE PIRATES
by MILTON CANIFF
OBSERVE, RYAN, THE JAPANESE DESTROYERS MOVE ON THE SEAWARD SIDE OF THE CONVOY —TO PROTECT IT FROM AMERICAN SUBMARINES!
WE ATTACK FROM THE LAND SIDE — CAREFULLY CHOOSING A SUPPLY SHIP, RATHER THAN A TROOP TRANSPORT! THE DRAGON LADY MEANS TO SALVAGE SOME OF THOSE SUPPLIES!
THIS IS WHERE YOUR FANCY PHONOGRAPH COMES INTO PLAY, I PRESUME!
SO! THIS RECORDING WAS MADE AT STANDARD SPEED! THE LOUD SPEAKER AT OUR MASTHEAD PROJECTS THE SOUND INTO THE NIGHT! IT IS CHEAPER THAN AIRCRAFT!
ON THE JAPANESE SHIP...
RRRRNNNNOOOW
BRRNNNNOOOW
...AIR ATTACK! COMMENCE FIRING!
THE FLASHES OF ANTI-AIRCRAFT GUNS AND THEIR SEARCHLIGHTS GUIDE US — WHILE OUR BOATS PLANT SURFACE MINES TO SIMULATE BOMB EXPLOSIONS! THE GUNNERS ARE THINKING IN TERMS OF AIR ATTACK!... NOW WE RELEASE OUR TORPEDO JUNKS!

Panel 1: A PICKED CREW HAS ROWED ONE EXPLOSIVE-LADEN JUNK BEYOND THE PATH OF THE ONCOMING SUPPLY VESSEL... THE MEN SET THE FUSES ON THE MINES LASHED TO THE SIDE—THEN CAST OFF IN A SMALL BOAT...

Panel 2: ...TOWARD SHORE, THE SAME THING HAS HAPPENED... THE TWO JUNKS ARE TIED TOGETHER BY A STRONG TOW-LINE... WHEN THE BOW OF THE JAPANESE SHIP STRIKES THE HALF-SUBMERGED ROPE, THE MINE-BEARING JUNKS CONVERGE

Panel 4: THERE SHE BLOWS! / MOVE IN QUICKLY, BELOW THEIR ANGLE OF FIRE! WHILE THE CREW TAKES TO THE BOATS ON THE SHORE SIDE—WE GO UP OUR BOARDING LADDERS ON THE SEAWARD SIDE! ...GO!

Panel 1: OUR DYNAMITE JUNKS HIT THE ENEMY SUPPLY SHIP SQUARELY, MY COMMANDER! / THE JAPANESE WILL BE TAKING TO THEIR SMALL BOATS ON THE SEAWARD SIDE! GET MORE BOARDING LADDERS UP! WE RACE AGAINST TIME!

Panel 2: THE SHIP WILL BE CARRYING GOLD TO BRIBE NATIVE CHIEFS! IF YOU CANNOT OPEN THE SAFE, LOWER IT OVER THE SIDE TO OUR JUNKS!

Panel 3: BEHOLD! WE ARE ATTACKED BY A CHINESE RABBLE! SHOOT DOWN THE LEADERS!

Panel 4: SHOULDN'T BOTHER A LADY WHEN SHE'S BUSY!

Panel 1: RYAN—WE MUST SILENCE THE WIRELESS BEFORE THE OPERATOR WARNS THE JAPANESE DESTROYERS IN THE CONVOY THAT WE ARE RAIDING THIS SUPPLY SHIP! / ...OKAY, BEAUTIFUL! IF I PICK UP A GOOD DANCE BAND I'LL GIVE YOU A JINGLE!

Panel 2: ...SHIP IS SETTLING TO PORT... CREW TAKING TO BOATS, UNCERTAIN WHETHER MINES OR TORPEDOES CAUSED EXPLOSION!

Panel 3: ...BUT IT IS NO ORDINARY ATTACK... WE ARE BEING BOARD---

Panel 4: SRT-GRN-EEEP... AND THUS WE CONCLUDE OUR TRAVEL PROGRAM FOR THE KIDDIES...THIS IS YOUR UNCLE PAT, SPEAKING TO YOU FROM OUR STUDIOS HIGH ATOP JERRY'S TAVERN... GOOD NIGHT, MY LITTLE FRIENDS!

OTHER CANIFF BOOKS FROM NBM:

TERRY & THE PIRATES COLLECTOR'S EDITION SPECIAL SALE!
Beautiful hardbound volumes, gold stamped, 320 pp. each, jacketed. Normally $36.50 each; NOW ONLY $19.95!
Volumes remaining: 7 (1940-'41), 8 ('41-'42), 11 ('44-'45), 12 ('45-'46).

"MILTON CANIFF, REMBRANDT OF THE COMIC STRIP"
Biography of Caniff with an introduction by comics historian Rick Marschall, editor of Nemo. Many rare illustrations and stunning blow-ups of Caniff's art.
Paperback, 64 pp., 8½x11: $6.95

GET 'EM HOT OFF THE PRESS! SUBSCRIBE!
This Terry & the Pirates reprint is quarterly like clockwork. Make sure to get each new volume hot off the press, sent in a sturdy carton mailer. You can start with any volume, past or future!
$25 for 4 volumes

MISSING ANY PAST VOLUMES?
Vol. 1 Welcome to China (1934) $6.95
Vol. 2 Marooned with Burma (1935) $5.95
Vol. 3 Dragon Lady's Revenge (1936) $5.95
Vol. 4 Getting Snared (1936-37) $5.95
Vol. 5 Shanghaied (1937) $5.95
Vol. 6 The Warlord Klang (1937-38) $6.95
Vol. 7 The Hunter (1938) $6.95
Vol. 8 The Baron (1938-39) $6.95
Vol. 9 Feminine Venom (1939) $6.95
Vol. 10 Network of Intrigue (1939-40) $6.95
Vol. 11 Gal Got Our Pal (1940) $6.95
Vol. 12 Flying Ace Dude (1940-41) $6.95
Vol. 13 "Into the Frying Pan..." (1941) $6.95
Vol. 14 Raven... (1941) $6.95

HANDSOME SLIPCASED SETS
4 volumes in each for a total of 256 pages of intense reading, slipcased in a leathery cloth, gold-stamped with the Terry logo.
Vols. 1-4: $29.50
Vols. 5-8: $29.50
Vols. 9-12: $29.50
SLIPCASE ALONE: $7.50

P&H: Add $2 first item, $1 each addt'l.
No P&H on subscriptions!

NBM
35-53 70th St.
Jackson Heights, NY 11372

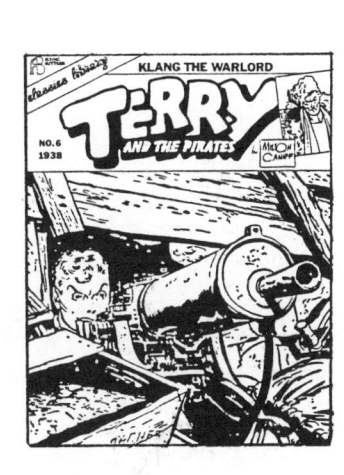

Flying Buttress Classics Library
presents:
The Complete 1924-1943
WASH TUBBS
AND CAPTAIN EASY SOLDIER OF FORTUNE by Roy Crane

This classic adventure strip which inspired many to come is now being fully reprinted in quarterly volumes of 192 pages each, including the infectiously dynamic adventures of Captain Easy in his own full Sunday pages with stunning artwork by Crane, this reprint will run a total of 18 volumes. Available in a beautifully gold-stamped library hardcover edition with mounted art or in trade paperback.
Each volume: 8½x11, 192 pp., B&W.
Hardcover: $32.50.
Paperback: $16.95.

SUBSCRIBE!
Get any 4 hardcovers for only $80 (*$130 separately*), **or any 4 paperbacks for $50** (*$67.80 separately*).
No postage and handling on subs!

10 volumes available (1924-1936)

NBM • 35-53 70th St. • Jackson Heights NY 11372